Thomas Cooper

The paradise of martyrs: A faith rhyme

Part first in five books

Thomas Cooper

The paradise of martyrs: A faith rhyme
Part first in five books

ISBN/EAN: 9783337259471

Printed in Europe, USA, Canada, Australia, Japan

Cover: Foto ©Andreas Hilbeck / pixelio.de

More available books at **www.hansebooks.com**

THE

PARADISE OF MARTYRS:

A Faith Rhyme.

PART FIRST.—IN FIVE BOOKS.

BY

THOMAS COOPER,

AUTHOR OF "THE PURGATORY OF SUICIDES; A PRISON RHYME,"
ETC., ETC., ETC.

LONDON:

HODDER AND STOUGHTON,

27, PATERNOSTER ROW.

MDCCCLXXIII.

PREFACE.

BEFORE my Prison-Rhyme, "The Purgatory of Suicides," was finished—thirty years ago—I promised myself to write "The Paradise of Martyrs." A busy life has prevented me from trying to fulfil my promise, in any shape, until very lately. And, even now, I offer but half of my purposed Faith-Rhyme to the world—I mean to the kind people who care to read it. If I do not live to write the other half, these five books are complete in themselves, and will serve to shew what my purpose was ; and, perhaps, to over-satisfy many who have, for years, urged me to the fulfilment of my promise.

At sixty-eight, one ceases to be sanguine, if not to care, about literary success. I quite expect the critics will cry out, "What tame stuff is this com-pared with 'the Purgatory'!" But I shall take no offence, nor fret with chagrin. My quiet consolation will be that my " Paradise" is *happier* than my " Purgatory." It is the fruit, not of a mind struggling with doubt in a gloomy prison ; but of a heart, thank God! throbbing with gratitude to Him for restoration to Christian faith and Christian life, and daily intent on spreading that faith and life in the hearts of others.

I have not burthened my poem with numerous Notes, because people do not read pages of Notes now-a-days. The few I have added to each Book seemed to be necessary ; and that is the only reason why they appear.

THOMAS COOPER.

TO WILLIAM EDWARD FORSTER.

I DEDICATE this book to you who sought
Me out, when you had read my Prison-Rhyme—
Disdainful of what cowards and serviles thought
Of one who had worn the fetters for no crime—
But only had lived and striven before his time,
And let his heart impel him to the deed
Of championship defiant for the Poor,
Their right to live by labour, and be freed
Indeed—not mocked with freedom—on the shore
Where Freedom hath her boast.

     Kindness doth breed
Grateful remembrance in the inmost core
Of true men's hearts, when done to them in need.
Let me be named with those who ne'er forget
A kindness : reckoning it a great life-debt.

 My friend, our lot in stormful time is cast ;
And who to God and Conscience, reverent, own
Inviolable fealty should hold fast
Each other's hands, in spite of peasants' frown
Or nobles'. Your great path of Duty strown
With difficulty may be for many a day ;
And, sometimes, you may have to strive alone ;
But shoulder to shoulder with you, in the fray.

Shall stand the good and true, when heat is gone,
And party spleen,—and all perceive dismay
At serried foes doth never cast you down,
Nor difficulty your patient courage allay ;
But your consistent course to all men shews
What you are now you will be to Life's close.

I shall not live to see your toil complete ;
But know your steady aim to the end will be
Still to preserve Old England the firm seat
Of grandest freedom, and to give the key
Of knowledge unto all.   Felicity
The highest that our fatherland can share
You wish to see her win : that every child
Be trained so wisely and well, it may with care
The laws which freemen love keep undefiled,
Nor heedless be of holier laws that bear
The Maker's fiat.   Toiling, unbeguiled
By smiles, unquelled by frowns, the pearl still wear
Of an unsullied conscience, and your joy,
Throughout Life's path, no censure shall destroy !

THE PARADISE OF MARTYRS.

B.OOK I.

I.

FULL fleetly, thirty years of strife have flown

Since I—the dreamer—in yon prison-hold,

Struck my lone harp of rude and cheerless tone,

With hand unskilful, and perchance, too bold

For dainty ears that love the chords of gold,

Touched by sleek charmers, known by accent bland

And silken smile; and deem your rhyming scold

Of Power and Privilege; a fiery brand

That lordly men should quench, in this old queenly land.

I

2.

Full fleetly fly the years! Gray Age hath come,
And Mind is slow,—for blood and brain are chilled,
And Memory maunders, or her tongue is dumb
As death, when she should tell what forms have filled
The soul with awe—what joys or throes have thrilled
The heart—throughout Life's changeful day:
A task that, once, young Memory deftly trilled,
And lightly, as a laughing child at play,
Till dull Age came, and chid the happy power away!

3.

Old Age hath come, and my long-chosen task
Is unfulfilled—for, I have loitered long
As well as chosen. Yet a man may ask,
And wisely, if the loitering hath been wrong:
Fools gather wisdom, and the weak grow strong,
Not seldom, by delay: good thoughts have grown
Where evil flourished. When the fitful throng
And tempest of our noon of life are gone,
The calm oft comes, in glory, with the setting sun.—

4.

Almighty and all-glorious Lord of all!

Eternal Source of life, and Fount of light!

A poor, dark wanderer, at Thy feet I fall—

Forgiving Father, at Thy feet! Thy bright

Pervading Presence in the darksome night

Of wandering watched me: Thou wert ever near,

Although I owned Thee not, and from Thy sight

Afar I fled, soul-palsied with the fear

That there was nought beyond the tomb: that dread
    so drear!

5.

O God! I thank Thee that I never lost

Heart-worship for Thy Son—the Christ—the Blest!

That, while my reason wandered, driven and tost

From doubt to deeper doubt, until the quest

For Truth oft ended in Despair's unrest—

The torturous, wild unrest of fell Despair!—

Yet, in my gloom, that sorrowing Visage drest

In rays of moral beauty seemed to share

My sorrow, and to say—"Come hither! learn to bear

6.

" My yoke, poor wanderer, and thou shalt find rest :

Rest from vain labour : from thy spirit's pain—

Swift ease : come hither, to thy Saviour's breast ! "

Sweet Lord, I come ! my labour hath been vain :

My search for rest.   Unbind my heavy chain

Of sin : release me, Saviour, with Thy good

And powerful hand : wash out my guilty stain

Of rebel pride in Thy atoning blood !

In brokenness of heart, I come—my Lord—my God !

7.

Thou givest peace not as the world doth give !

To me Thy peace be given—that, while this thread

Of mortal life is spun, my soul may live

For Thee alone ; and I may humbly tread

My fatherland, from side to side, and spread

Thy truth.   Help me to preach it to the Poor

Who strive to think out, while they toil for bread,

The mystery of existence, and explore

That sea's vast bounds where mightiest thinkers ne'er

found shore !

8.

Thou seest them, pitying Father, in their doubt

And darkness!   And Thy just and sovereign gaze

Is fixt upon the mimesters who beclout

Themselves anew with rags of Rome, and raise,

Once more, for idol, with old pomps, and blaze

Of gold, and bannered splendours, and the sheen

Of lamps and candles, and the fragrant praise

Of incensed-chaunt, their starry-vestured Queen—

The lowly mother of the lowly Nazarene !

9.

The toiling thousands grope for saving truth,

And yearn to find ;—but ye seek not to save

Your untaught brethren with the words of ruth

And tenderness.   It is for altars brave,

And gay bedizenments, ye hotly crave :

Dalmatica, and chasuble, and cope,

Biretta, rubied cross, and ivoried stave

Episcopal :—to have these toys ye hope—

But, for Christ's truth, still let the toiling thousands

grope !

10.

Out on your childish greed for gew-gaws : toys

On which your martyred sires could scarcely look

Without a frown !   Are there no nobler joys

Within your grasp ?   Have ye for these forsook

The simple truths your fathers loved ? They shook

The Romish slavery off; and freedom, then,

Truly became your birthright : if ye brook

Meekly the Papal yoke to wear again,

Will your sons look ye in the face, and call ye—Men?

11.

The toiling thousands think upon the Past,

And its fierce martyr-fires ; and, while they yearn

To fathom Mind's deep mysteries, feel no haste

To look for light from darkness, or to learn

Lessons from hildings who deserve their scorn.

In homely tongue, they ask—"No better tools

For digging out the Truth do doctors earn

Than these, within their costly halls and schools ?

Do they build colleges to breed and foster fools ? "

12.

And then they settle down in doubt, or try

A resting-place in restless doubt to find

In vain : for, still, the agonising cry,

Aloud, is heard of Doubt half-maddening mind ;

And, still, they grope for Truth—the inly blind !

Or, in disgust, they give up thinking ;—game

And bet, like lords ! on horses ; and behind

Cast care and conscience ; or the viler drame

Play out of sottishness and sensualism and shame !

13.

O for the gift to earth of some great souls !

O for the birth of men to found a new

And nobler chivalry than decks the rolls

Of real or mimic war !   O that a few .

Among the Schooled and Privileged would thew

Their wills with high resolve, and grandly rise

To throw their hearts among the crowd,—the True

To champion, and cast down the forms of Lies—

Warriors for Good, old Evil's power to antagonize !

14.

Not dead to noble sympathies, and words

Fraternal, are the crowd that doubt, and dare

The depths of sin. In every heart are chords

That vibrate to the touch of humblest player

Or lordliest, if responding chords declare

Their touch is truly human. Patrons smart

And scented,—teachers with the lofty air

Of condescension, seem to the stalwart, swart,

And sturdy sons of Labour—Things without a heart.

15.

How long will this new dotage last—your strife

To re-enthrone old Priestcraft ? Do ye dream

That ye can veritably restore to life

The dead putrescence ? 'Midst the whirl of steam,

The speed of telegraphs, and lightning-gleam

Of knowledge which proclaims the Reign of Law,

Will toiling men a truth your bold tale deem

That ye can make your Maker ; and with awe

Bow down, in trembling fear of your anathema ?

16.

They neither fear ye, nor your curse : your creed

Is monstrous to their common sense : they pine

For rest in Truth, not mockery.   Strive to lead

The toiling crowd to reverence and enshrine

The Real Presence of the Lord Divine

Within their hearts, and let your acts reveal

That, while ye say ye love the Lord benign,

Ye truly serve Him ; and, with grateful zeal,

Devout, responsive crowds will welcome your appeal.—

17.

The night falls fast, and finds me brooding thus

O'er evils that afflict my fatherland :—

The night falls fast, yet brightly luminous

Beam out the cotton mills that round me stand,

Where garish gas turns night to day ; and hand,

And eye, and mind of myriad toilers win

The wealth of England, but cannot command

A certainty of bread,—though, for her sin,

Woman, like man, doth weave, and watch, and toil,

and spin.

18.

Their toil now ceases, and my toil comes next.

I gather them around me, and essay

To teach them how to solve the "questions vext"

That puzzle and perplex them through the day,

Amid the din of wheels, and sweat and fray

Of factory life.   Some yawn with weariness;

Some frown ; some sneer ; some seem but clods of

  clay ;

But some look all aglow with bright excess

Of rapt conviction which their minds doth overbless.

19.

My task ends all too soon.   I wish the hours

Could stand; or these till morn could sit, and hear,

And think.   But drowsiness their frames o'erpowers;

And, ere day dawns, they must the call austere

O', the factory-bell obey—Toil's chanticleer !

But, let it cheer my heart that, through each week,

I can my task pursue,—although the sere

And yellow leaf be mine ;—and freely speak—

Fearing no frowns, nor listening for applauses sleek.

20.

Whathand—whatstrangerhand—shall closethese eyes,

I cannot know,—or who stretch out my feet ;

What hushèd voice say—" A breathless corpse he lies,

His wanderings o'er : prepare the winding-sheet ! "

Anxious to make my pilgrimage complete,

I will work on, rejoicing, let betide.

What may, on earth. I covet the bright seat

He promised them that love Him, close beside

His throne of love—my glorious Lord, the Crucified !

21.

I fear, no longer, that my being destroyed

Shall be, when men shall lay this body low ;

That Mind shall perish in the mindless void,

And I shall cease to think, and feel, and know,

Although for ever there shall be the glow

Of thought and feeling in God's Universe.

The risen Christ with life shall re-endow

My soul ; and ne'er shall sin again amerce

My Christ-enfranchised being with Death's benumbing
    curse.

22,

For ever with my Lord, who said, " I am
The Resurrection and the Life," I trust
To be ; and to that trust I cleave.   Still maim
And blind is Mind, and blind and maim it must
Remain, how Mind shall live when dust to dust
Returns.   But, since we cannot know the state
Beyond the grave, all-unperturbed robust
And patient souls should wait—unfaltering wait,
And calmly,—for the spirit-life emancipate.—

23.

Midnight hath come.   I would that gentle sleep
Would visit me ; but seldom comes repose,
Now age is raught.   Thought the long watch doth keep,
To wander o'er the Past, with operose
And feeble steps, or vainly seeks to unclose
The barriers of the Future, till the brain
Is worn and wildered.   Then, the startled doze
Of nervousness succeeds, or, hours of pain ;
And, seldom, o'er the sense, Sleep spreads her blissful
    reign.

24.

I sought for slumber, and, unwontedly,

Sweet Slumber, swiftly, on my eyelids laid

Her hand, full gently—as, on mother's knee,

A gentle mother's hand is softly stayed

Upon her helpless child.

Again, I strayed—

Or seemed to stray—in spirit, beyond the bound

Of earthly life : no longer, now, affrayed

With visioned forms that agonized and frowned

With rage, or sat in emblemed pomp, enthroned and

crowned.[1]

25.

I dreamed I walked the " land of pure delight,

Where everlasting spring abides, and never

Wither the flowers ; " where neither worm nor blight

Attaints their bloom, for ever and for ever : /

Where neither sin nor death again can sever

The noble Army of Martyrs from their Lord,

Or unto pain again their souls deliver.

To Jesus' heaven of bliss, it seemed, I soared,

Where myriads of His saints God and the Lamb adored.

26.

But I knew not 'twas heaven, as first I woke—

Or seemed to wake—when I escaped from earth.

Upon my spiritual sight a vision broke

So like the "dear, dear land"* that gave me birth,—

So like the woods, and vales, and hills where mirth

And glee were rife in childhood,—that it seemed

I had but lately left my Mother's hearth

To wander forth, and gather flowers that gleamed

With strange, unearthly splendour. Thus I dimly dreamed.

27.

I wandered in the pathway of a wood

Where delicatest wind-flowers round me lay,

Like snow new fall'n ; and spring-born bluebells stood,

In slender tallness, peering o'er the array

Of humble violets and pied pansies gay,

With mimic pride ; while, waving overhead,

Young silken beech-leaves and slim birchen-spray

Fleckt the pure light that from above was shed ;

And still I seemed some well-known woodland path to
    thread.

28.

Yet, evermore, methought, no earthly hue

The trees and flowers displayed ; while neither cloud

Nor shade there seemed to be.   And, soon, a new

And dazzling light revealed a smiling crowd

Of childlike forms—but, dimness, like a shroud,

Swiftly enwrapped the vision ; and terrene,

Again, seemed all things.   Then, arose a proud

And terraced pile of mountains ever green ;

And I sped on to reach them, through a lowlier scene.

29.

Soft hills sloped gently towards a verdant vale :

Like the loved hills that bound thy vale, O Trent !—

And, midway, in the valley wound the trail

Of a bright river, like a filament

Of sparkling silver.   On its banks were blent

Trent's floral riches—as I did misdeem—

The vernal crocus prankt with transient

And blushing beauty ; cranesbill's sky-born gleam

Intense—looking like eyes of angels, in my dream ;

30.

The huge-leaved butter-bur, with flowers so quaint;

Clustered marsh-marigolds that did bedaze

My eyes, till I withdrew them by constraint ;

And still more dazzling was the golden blaze

Of water-lilies.
                        Now, again, with rays

Of light encircled, childlike creatures smiled

Upon me.   Unaffrayed, but in amaze

I stood ; for none looked like an earth-born child :

They seemed too pure for souls derived from men defiled.

31.

"What are ye, beauteous things?" methought I spake.

Silent, they beckoned me with smiles of grace ;

And dimness soon again seemed to o'ertake

My vision—for, they faded till no trace

Remained of their bright forms.   I trod, apace,

The flowery vale, with strong desire to climb

The terraced mountains ; but the winning face

Of some fair flower, so dear to childhood's time,

Brought back my thoughts, in wonder still, to childhood's
        clime.

32.

What virgin purity the flowers that grew
Nigh the bright winding river seemed to wear—
Sweet cicely, and meadow-sweet, and rue!
And cuckoo-flowers and chervils bloomed so fair,
They were as magnets to my eyes; and there
I lingered, when I thought to hasten on
And climb the mountains' sides to see what rare
Large prospect from their summits might be won
Of that rich floral realm so sweetly halcyon.

33.

I stooped to pluck a lily from the marge
Of the fair river, since it grew so near,
And bloomed so dazzling white and grandly large;
But, ere I touched it, suddenly in my ear
Streamed music, soft as whispers, and yet clear
And sweet as that sweet "Pastoral Symphony"
Oft heard on earth—the dulcet harbinger
Of lofty praise, and holy and heavenly glee:
Charmed prelude to the burst of angel minstrelsy.

34.

Still sweeter grew the sounds, and fairer bloomed
The flowers, till rapt thoughts strengthened that I trode
No earthly soil, but precincts to bliss-doomed,
Celestial realms, where vigour is bestowed
On franchised souls to fit them for their load
Of bliss—the " weight of glory " which they bear—
" Far more exceeding and eternal,"—who see God:
They who eternal joys beyond compare
Esteem, with light affliction saints on earth may share.

35.

The thought that I was heir of bliss so great,
And that earth's life of sin and sorrow and pain
Was past, began, well-nigh, to tribulate
The soul with ecstasy: an overgain
Of bliss, it seemed, for one who knew the stain
Of sin—though all forgiven—henceforth to dwell
With endless joy.   But soon, in tuneful strain,
Some unseen choral band, with jubilant swell,
Above, around me, pealed these words delectable :—

36.

"Spirit, rejoice! thy mortal life is past :

This land of living light no cloud can gloom :

Sin cannot reach it, with her fatal blast :

Here flowers can never fade, but ever bloom :

Here pain, or sin-bred anguish cannot come :

Death vanquisheth Man's dust, but not the soul :

Man's spirit is no tenant of the tomb—

No prisoner to the grave.   Rejoice, thy dole

Is ended ; and thy soul hath reached her happy goal !

37.

"Welcome, new heritor of bliss! begin

To enter on thy rest.   Let no alloy,

Or thought that thou hast known the stain of sin,

Lessen thy rapture, or thy bliss destroy.

Onward, and prove the fulness of that joy

Thy Saviour promised.   He thy debt hath paid,

And thou art free !   Prepare for blest employ

Through countless ages !   Joys that never fade

Are thine : increasing joys thy essence shall pervade!

38.

"Onward, and join the dear companions blest
Thou soon shalt meet: they who thy Saviour loved
And served, and openly His Name confessed;
Nor to deny their Lord were weakly moved
When bad men threatened, but were faithful proved
Through lives of suffering, and in deaths of shame:
They who proclaimed that holy truth behooved
Their bodies should be given unto the flame
With joyous haste, so they might homage Jesus' Name!"

39.

The glittering band of childlike creatures beamed
Above me, as the jubilant strain surceased,
That, now I knew, was theirs. Then, as I dreamed,
They vanished; and I entered on glad quest
For some I yearned to see among the Blest—
Some who the martyr's crown obtained by faith,
In fiery flames, and nobly did attest
The power of faith to draw the sting of death:
Who died exulting in their Lord with their last breath!

40.

My fatherland's intrepid martyrs were

The souls I longed to meet ; and wish devout

I felt to gaze on reverend Latimer,—

The memory of whose nobleness oft wrought

Deep love within me, in my days of doubt

And wandering. Forthwith, as in dungeoned plight,[3]

The soul with intellective power seemed fraught

To realize her wish ; and, clothed with light,

The grand old martyr was revealed unto my sight !

41.

And with him Ridley walked, in radiant dress

Of pure white robes ; and garland-crowns they wore

Of flowers that did transcend in beauteousness

And splendour the fair flowers upon the shore

Of the bright river, though I deemed, before,

These were all-peerless.   Hand in hand appeared

The shining martyrs.   As, for Christ, of yore,

To burn together they nor shrunk, nor feared,

So were they to each other, now, in bliss endeared.

42.

That his brave death-words rose within my mind,

Seemed quickly known unto the martyred sire;

And, that I feared their failure, he divined :

Whereat—unknowing that blest souls in higher

Ascents of purity the power acquire

To read their brethren's thought—I, speechless, stood

In wonder.   Bravely, as if he marched the fire

Again to welcome with old hardihood,

He upward glanced, and thus his faith unshaken

shewed :—

43.

"Fear not, young heir of heaven ! harbour no doubt

That Truth shall triumph. Falsehood's fellest power

The candle never shall again put out

We lighted up for England, in that hour

We dared the flame,—while, 'mong the crowds from tower

And hall and cloister, some that saw the deed

With fear at first, felt soon they would not cower

'Fore tenfold tortures ; and, in flames, did read

This truth: the 'Martyrs' blood shall be the Church's seed !'

44.

" Fear not for Truth—for Christ's own glorious Truth!

Falsehood may, yet, put forth spasmodic force,

Again and oft, and vaunt her purity and youth,

Though every step of her foul crooked course

Speaks her decrepit.   Despots may endorse

Her lies for truth, to prop their crumbling thrones ;

And fools the gay-trickt harridan may nurse

And fondle ; but rotten are her very bones :

Her scrannel songs scarce serve to drown her dying

groans.

45.

" Onward, young heir of Jesus' happy heaven !

We go on messages of mercy sweet,

Once more, to earth : such blest employ hath given

The Lamb to His glad saints.   Thee soon shall greet

Dear souls familiar by their names : thy meet

And loving teachers : till a convoy bright

Of angels, swift, shall bring thee to the feet

Of Jesus glorified, amid His saints in white ;

And thou shalt worship with them in supernal light!"

46.

Away, they sped!—the shining Martyr pair,—
On their blest errand, with most eager love,
To do their loving Master's will.   To share
Their work, methought, I coveted, and strove
To follow them.   But, sweetest strains above,
Around me swelled, until I sank o'erpowered
With ecstasy of sweetness—though I longed to
    prove
The service of that heaven where saints adored,
In myriad throngs of love, their glorious risen Lord.

47.

"Onward, still onward!"—did the sweet chaunt swell,
From unseen choristers—" Thou wilt not find
Thy rest in rapture.   They on earth who dwell
Miss their chief happiness because, with blind
Perception of true bliss, they stay behind
To reap the lesser joys that virtue gives,
And toil not for the greater.   God designed
The soul for duty ; and he who, tireless, strives
To render duteous service unto God derives

48.

" Still higher bliss from every duteous deed.

God did engraft in moral natures sense

Of praise and blame ; and holiest natures feed

On consciousness of duty done, and thence

Derive, for God's sweet service, more intense

And holy and earnest zeal : blest avarice

It is, to covet largest opulence

Of zeal for duty : who rest in rapture miss

True good : eternal service is eternal bliss ! "

49.

And, now, grew visible a glorious band

Of spirits I seemed intuitively to know :

The gallant Martyrs of my fatherland :

Our noble Cobham ; Hooper, the unyielding foe

Of slavish pomps ; young Bilney, with faith's glow

Exultant ; praying Bradford—devotee

So true and holy ; Philpot, with the brow

Of high intelligence ; Anne Askew, she

Who cheered her fellow-sufferers with such holy glee ;

50.

And melancholy Mary's victims: Rogers, first
On whom her priests, watching like wolves for prey,
Contrived to slake their sanguinary thirst ;
Saunders, who burnt at Coventry ; and they—
A hero-crowd besides—who, in the day
Of vengeful Gardiner, and power of Rome
Retrieved, and Bonner's savage zeal to slay,—
In Smithfield left their ashes, without gloom
Clasping the flames, triumphing in their fiery doom.

51.

With these came Bainham, who, when fire had raged
And burned his nether limbs, aloud proclaimed
"This is a bed of roses!"—so assuaged
His faith fierce pain!   The weaver humble-named,
Too,—Tomkins,—'neath whose wrist a taper flamed,
Held by brute Bonner, who thus vainly thought
To fright his victim; Hawkes, who threw his maimed
And burning arms aloft, to quell the doubt
Of trembling lovers who this sign of him had sought ;

52.

Hunter, the gentle boy whose mother and sire
Rejoiced that God to them so brave a child
Had given, to bear Him witness in the fire;
Farrar, who, at Caermarthen, his foes foiled
So stoutly in the flames; Tindal, who toiled
For future ages, and received the crown
Of martyrdom,—by treachery foul beguiled;
With steadfast Lambert, who the tiger frown
Undaunted bore of Henry seated on his throne.

53.

Brave Rowland Taylor with this martyred host
Came nobly on.   But there was one aside
Who walked, as if for him there were no boast
Among his brethren—no exultant pride:
'Twas Cranmer, seeming with himself to chide,
Even in heaven!   With these came many more
Who burned in England; while, great souls allied
In faith and fervour, whom in her heart's core
Of reverence faithful Scotland long hath proudly bore,

54.

Came with them : noble Hamilton, whom proud

And sensual Beatoun dragged to death, but fell,

Himself a victim to his country's loud

Demand for vengeance ; holy Wishart, well

And worthily ranked with martyrs vincible

By neither man nor demon ; Renwick bold ;

With crowds whom Power and Priestcraft could not

    quell :

The men who did the Solemn Covenant hold

As sacred :—men of high, heroic, martyr mould.

55.

I saw this shining host, and knew the chaunt

Was theirs ; and one upraised me with a smile ;

And on I journeyed with them, while descant

They joined, how holy joys the spirit thrill

That thirsts some higher duty to fulfil,

- Nor counts on rapture for reward, or ease,

    Or rest, but evermore to service still

    Aspires ; and how the soul new service sees

Before it, ever ; and thus eternal pleasures please.

56.

And then, conversing of the work they loved,

They told each other of the sights just seen

On earth,—for, soon, my wistful spirit proved

That these glad souls to mother Earth had been,

To cheer God's children in their earthly teen,—

And how they loved the loving sweet employ :

And then, by turns, they pictured, each, some scene

Of holy suffering and of holy joy,

And patient faith and trust no suffering could destroy.

57.

Some told of mother's love, and watchings pale,

Beside a dying child ; and some pourtrayed

The dread heartbrokenness that bowed a frail

Old man whom Death had robbed of all the aid—

The earthly aid—he had, and lowly laid

His loving life-companion in the grave ;

While some rehearsed how sorrow preyed

Upon the hearts of children who, to save

Their dying parents, watched and waited with devo-

tion brave.

58.

And some depictured how a virgin flower
Of loveliness no words could tell declined
Upon its fragile stem, from hour to hour—
A loving maid beloved : two intertwined
And beauteous natures : in the youth the mind,
And in the maid the form, being fair as heaven;
And how she slept in death, and the youth pined
Away in grief, for that all bliss seemed given
With her on earth: with her all bliss away was riven!

59.

The shipwrecked sailor, in the ocean wide—
Others described—and how his last lorn prayer
Was for his bosom's love, the tender bride
He left on land, far off—the home so fair
He decked so daintily, with shells so rare
And foreign beauteous things ; and how the dread
Mysterious boding in her heart despair
Succeeds, and daily her tears for him are shed,
Long ere some lone survivor tells her he is dead.

60.

And others told of negro slaves, and pain
And torture meekly borne by many a thrall
Who never breathed offence to those for gain
Who bought and sold him, but obeyed their call
To wait and toil when he could scarcely crawl
To do their fiendish bidding.   Others shewed
How some bore ignominy that would not fall
Before men's idols, though it seemed the load
Would crush them : still the knee to Baal they never
    bowed.

61.

The noble courage, in the Battle of Life,
Of peaceful warriors—others eulogised ;
The men who with vindictiveness and strife
And hate and malice, daily agonised ;
And strove to show mankind howe'er they prized
Red Victory's brow with laurel chaplet green,
Her real features were the Fiend's disguised.
And then they shewed how all who tried to wean
Men from War's madness suffered persecution keen.

62.

With loving grief—such grief as saints can feel
In heaven—some told of hard oppression borne
By a poor widow, toiling at the wheel
Or loom, with hungered frame, sore weary and worn,
To keep her fatherless ones from sin and scorn,—
Yet meeting sympathy from none—but sneers
From bestial tempters she doth meekly spurn.
And how the meek one leans on Him Who hears
His saints' low cry, and bottles up His tried ones'
    tears.

63.

And then they spoke of heavenly condolence
They bore to sorrowers : strength to fortify
The suffering with belief in Providence
That fills the cup of grief and trial nigh
Unto the brim in wisdom, and doth try
His saints in love, but never lets the cup
Run o'er; that counts each tear, that hears each sigh,
Of all His contrite ones ; and, when they droop,
Sends heavenly help to bear their fainting spirits up.

64.

Of resignation, and of steadfast faith

When bad men persecute the good, and rage

And threaten them with chains and torturous death,

They told ;—and how, on holy embassage

They went to bear such help, their lineage

Of suffering rendering them the bearers meet.

And gratefully, they said—Mind could not gauge

The Love Divine that sent them forth to greet

And strengthen struggling saints by earthly foes beset;

65.

And that themselves, thus, with the Paraclete

Divine should share the work of comforting

God's saints was a reward ineffably sweet ;

And had they known what the Eternal King

Designed them for, it would have drawn the sting

Of torture in their martyrdom till praise

Had filled their souls ; and, like a bird on wing,

Each would have soared, exultant, with glad lays,

Above all thought of pain, in the devouring blaze !

66.

Thus while they held sweet descant, glode
Around us, oft, bands of the bright young quire
I saw when first I seemed the blest abode
Of saints to enter ; and I felt desire
Grow strong to know them.   Ne'er seemed they to tire ;
But ever floated on, with rapturous eyne
Betokening how they did the speech admire
Of God's glad martyrs, who the scheme benign
Extolled that did to them sweet ministering work assign.

67.

Ere I could ask, one answered my thought's quest.
" These are," said he, " but scanty companies
Of that great myriad army of the Blest
Of which they all are numbered.   Hither, when hies
A soul from earth, these meet it, and surprise
The welcome soul with sounds and looks of love,
And thus prepare it for the exercise
Of all the powers within its essence wove
By the Great Maker, that it may for ever prove

68.

"The blessedness of being, which God hath given.

These are the souls of infants : they of whom

The Saviour said of such the kingdom of heaven

Is.   Deem thou not He meant they hither come

As if heaven were all infants' bright heirloom

By native right of innocency.   Each soul

From Adam born is born in sin ; and doom

Of sin these 'scape, because Christ suffered dole

For them, and makes, by grace, their sin-grained spirits

whole.

69.

"Of such the kingdom of heaven is ; and young

They are for ever !   Thus, by Divine decree,

They who by actual sin of thought or tongue

Were never stained do first salute the free

And happy souls who join our jubilee

In heaven.   Old sin-stained earth they visit never,

Since sin or guilt they never knew : while we

Revisit sin's abode : the Great Life-giver

Thus serving, thus His service blest enjoying ever !"

70.

Soon seemed we to have raught the mountains green,

And up their terraced sides, untoiling, climbed,

Beholding myriad forms so bright, the sheen

Of all earth's gold and gems would have been dimmed

Beside their beauty.   Countenances sublimed

From mortal care and fear and doubt they wore ;

And, as they clomb the mountains, sweetly hymned

Their grateful joy, their earthly fight being o'er,

Of sin the stain and torture they should know no more.

71.

They sung not praise because from fiery flame,

Or fiercer bodily pain, they were set free,—

Although they out of great tribulation came ;—

But joyous hymns they sung, set to the key

Of purest love, because their leprosy

Of guilt was cleansed, and o'er them sin's dread reign,—

By Him Who captive led captivity,— .

Was broken, never to be resumed again :

Thus, as they climbed, they sang their ever grateful
  strain :—

"We come, O God, from holy work on earth,

To adore in heaven Thy glorious majesty !—

Father of all, and Son who once had birth

'Mong sinful men, and Holy Spirit, Three

In One, the Triune God !—to bow the knee

With all for whom Christ's precious blood hath
    streamed,

And angels fair !—to join heaven's jubilee,

With all the fallen whom Thou hast redeemed,

And all on whom for aye Thy unbroken smile hath
    beamed !

73.

"For ever blessed be Thy Holy Name !

Great Giver of existence and of thought !

Let all Thy saints return Thee sweet acclaim

For all the wonders which Thy hand hath wrought—

For all the bliss with which our life is fraught—

For all Thy long-forbearance when the sway

Of rebel Sin we owned, and foully fought

Against Thy sovereign love, from day to day.

We bless Thee that Thou didst not cast our souls away!

76.

"We bless Thy Holy Name we never here
Shall grieve Thy holiness, indulge desire
Or thought of sin, or ever feel a fear
Of falling! Evermore in us the fire
Divine shall burn to love Thee, and acquire
Still holier zeal; for Thou wilt guide our aim
To serve Thee, while to Thee our souls aspire,
And still wilt feed in us the holy flame!
For ever and ever blessed be Thy Holy Name!"

77.

So sang the myriad shining forms that climbed
The mountains ever green. And, as I glanced
Along their ranks, I saw their steps were timed:
So that in triumph-march the hosts entranced
With joy, up by the terraces advanced,—
While newer hosts of shining ones, from earth,
Still more their numbers and their joys enhanced,—
For upward still they clomb, all sending forth
The pæans of their grateful joy and holy mirth.

78.

Lo! when the hosts the mountain heights had won,

How shall I tell the glory of my dream?—

The golden crystal walls before us shone—

Those lofty walls adorned with sparkling gem

Of every name; and those twelve gates with beam

Resplendent of one matchless pearl :—the blest

Apocalyptic vision God did deem

Him worthy of who on the loving breast

Of Christ, on earth, so often found a loving rest!

79.

The new Jerusalem—the home, I saw,

Of God's dear saints for whom the Lamb's own blood

Was shed; and on the angels gazed with awe,

Who, at the pearly gates o' the City of God,

In panoply of light, as keepers, stood.

I thought their eyes pierced through me—but, behold!

They oped the mighty gates; and, like a flood,

The Martyr-hosts—who in their Lord were bold—

Streamed in, with songs of triumph, on the floor of gold!

80.

I went not with them ; for methought the band

With which I marched, to whom heaven's realm

    was new,

Were marshalled by an angel with a wand

Of silver, till he other bands outdrew

From the great host ; and soon he loudly blew

The golden trumpet which hung by his side—

And forth from out the gates a convoy flew

Of wingëd seraphim, who smiling cried :

" The Lamb unto the marriage-supper calls the Bride !

81.

" Come in, ye blessed of the Lord, come in !

Receive the mansions by your Lord prepared :

The glorious Crown of Life ye now shall win !

His truth and love ye have on earth declared :

With Him the hate of wicked men ye shared :

And though ye were not called to prove your faith

In the fierce flames which His confessors dared,

Ye have been faithful in your lives, till death.

Come in ! receive from His own hands the blooming

    wreath

82.

"Of immortality.   Come in, come in,

Ye blessed of the Lord! receive your bright

Reward!—the crown of glory ye shall win!"—

And now we seemed upborne on bands of light

By the winged seraphim, with gentle flight,

Into the City of God, even to the throne

Of God and of the Lamb : into the sight,

All-glorified, of Him who wore the crown

Of thorns, but now gives crowns of life unto His own!

83.

Vision of holiest love, how shall I tell

Thy sweetness!—or the splendour of that brow,

Of awfullest majesty, for earthlings spell

In characters that men may read!   O may I know

That smile ineffable when hence I go

To meet my Judge!—but all earth's languaged lore

Could not my soul with potency endow

To tell my dream : all earth-made speech were poor

To unveil the glory that the King in His beauty wore!

84.

The plenitude of pardon for all sin :

Eternal freedom from all sin and stain :

Welcome to mansions that should now begin,

And never fail—eternal welcome !—Pain

For ever ended, under His sweet reign   ′

Of health, and light, and love, and bliss !—Largess

Of knowledge bounteous: things obscure made plain:

The soul become, in heaven, close auditress

Of the Eternal Word, whose accents overbless

85.

The high archangels, as the saints in light :

Rapt consciousness no ceasing there should be

Of His all-gladdening smile : no darkening night

Of error—but bright perpetuity

Of rectitude : the soul from wrong set free,

That growth in wisdom of His works and ways

Might fill her enlarging powers with ecstasy,—

So that all souls, for aye, should grateful raise

To the All-Blest, All-Blessing One, their gladsome
    praise !

86.

All mortal words are mean!   More, far, of love—
Love bliss-endowing, bliss-entrancing, dwelt
In that one look that, from the throne above,
Glanced on my soul, than all the soul hath felt
On earth of joys in tenderness that melt
Our nature.   And 'twas bliss ALL felt; and ALL,
In speechless awe of overbliss, now knelt,
And loved, and worshipped, while it seemed to appal
The soul to experience bliss so beatifical!

87.

Ten thousand times ten thousand harps of gold,
Tuned by the fingers of the angelic throng,
Forthwith began sweet prelude to unfold—
Harmonious prelude trumpets did prolong
Of cherub and seraph—to the choral song
Of all the host, unfallen and redeemed,
Of highest heaven.   What voices, strong and clear,
Led the vast choir?   They on whose foreheads
    beamed
The mark the Lamb had set: His Martyrs dia-
    demmed!

88

"Worthy the Lamb," they cried, "that once was slain

For sinful men—who hath redeemed us by

His blood!" "Worthy, O Lord, Thou art to

    reign "—

Responded myriad angels holy and high—

"Who didst Thyself the souls of sinners buy

From endless pain ; and didst Thy Father's rule

Of righteousness for ever justify!"

"We bow," the archangels cried, "at Thy footstool,

O co-eternal Son, divinely pitiful!"

89.

"O Father!" sang all heaven, "we laud Thy Name

For Thy eternal purpose made so clear

In giving Him to suffering and to shame—

Thy only begotten Son, so loved and dear

Unto Thy heart divine—who hath no peer

In all created life—Thy Son, who hath

In Thine own bosom ever dwelt, that here,

In this Thy heaven of love, men, saved by faith

In Him, might live : for ever saved from Thy just

    wrath!"

90.

"O Spirit Divine!" sang on the general host
Of men and angels, "we adore Thy pure
Long-suffering love for man! O Holy Ghost,
Who didst so long the sight of sin endure—
Whose purity hath striven the foul to cure,
And conquered!—by whose sovereign breath
Sinners were born again,—their forfeiture
Of heaven was cancelled,—and they found the path
Up hither, by Thy light: made heirs of heaven,
    through faith!"

91.

"Eternal Triune God!" sang ransomed men
And sinless babes, and principalities
And powers, and holy creatures with the ken
All-spiritual—the creatures full of eyes!—
And angel and archangel companies,
And cherubim and seraphim; and, from
The macrocosm of God, myriads of guise
And form man cannot name, devoutly come
To welcome God's loved saints to their eternal home:

92.

"Eternal Triune God! Who wert, and art,

And art to come! Thrice holy, sovereign One!

Thyself sole Life, who dost their life impart

To all that live—Thyself sole Mind, the boon

To know who giv'st to all that think—sole Sun,

The light who giv'st to all that live and feel—

Sole Strength, their strength who giv'st to all that on

The solid worlds or ether move—reveal

Thyself who dost, in glory and love unspeakable!

93.

" We hymn Thy everlasting love, O Lord!

Thy love which gives us happy life, in thought

And act, Thy will in doing, and the reward

For ever finding in our work. Full fraught

Are all Thy works with love; and, by Thee taught,

For ever, thus, we work in love, and find

Our bliss enlarging ever; nor shall aught

Restrain or bound the bliss Thou hast designed

For all that do Thy will: the bliss with service joined.

94.

"O God, our greatest bliss is that we love

Thee, and Thou lovest us.   And Thou hast made

Us capable of loving more, and wove

In all our natures powers that, well essayed

In Thy blest service, Thou wilt ever aid

And strengthen, till for higher service still

Our being is fitted, and our thoughts all stayed

On Thy perfections.   Father, let Thy will

Be done!   With that desire alone our spirits fill!

95.

"Thy will is happiness to all that live.

It was Thy everlasting love that moved

Thee to create, and happy life to give.

No other life Thou ever gav'st.   They roved

From blessedness to bale, and swiftly proved

Their folly, who misused the freedom fair

Thou didst endow them with: for, it behoved

All spiritual natures should be free,—to share

Thy blest approval, or Thy righteous blame to bear.

96.

" Thy wisdom, as Thy power and love, adored

For ever be, by all that think and know !

We see not all Thy purposes, O Lord !

Not yet—although throughout the ages grow

Our essences in knowledge—do they glow

With full perception of Thy works and ways.

All-perfect One, Thou hast no yoke-fellow !

Afar, full oft, in awe we stand and gaze,

Or sink beneath the effulgence of Thy glory's rays !

97.

" We see not all Thy purposes, or aim.

If through the ages Evil survive, though Good

For ever with it war, and no reclaim

For evil-doers be found ; if still the proud

Submit not to Thy rule, repentant bowed,

At length, 'fore Thy high will so holy and bright—

Thy all-wise will be done !   For us, no cloud

Can hide the truth that Thou art true ; and right

Are all Thy ways, O Holy Dweller in the Light !

98.

"We know Thy will is that, like Thee, we war
Unceasingly with evil, and condole
With those that suffer : that, to still the jar
Of disobedience in each human soul,
In Thy blest sight is blessed.   No control
We have o'er loftier essences that fell
From holiness and bliss. . If in the roll
Of ages, spiritual powers who now rebel
Shall to Thy love return—O Lord, it shall be well—

99.

" For, such return unto Thy arms of love—
Unto Thy heart, that yearns all being to bless—
Shall to Thy saints and angels grateful prove
Thy wisdom, in its depths, how fathomless !—
How perfectly the spotless, bright impress
Of love is stamped on Thy great government,
Through all Thy realms of life and boundlessness!—
O Thou who art alone all-prescient,
Thy holy will be done—O Lord, all-excellent !

100.

"Now round Thy throne again we grateful crowd,
And join our praise for all Thy goodness past,
Present, to come ;—for all, with which endowed
Of intellect and strength, we feel.Thou hast
Blest our existence!   Giver of goodness vast,
Interminable, as of life, we hymn
The wondrous love with which Thou hast embraced
Alike, the wanderers who Thy gifts bedim,
But seek forgiveness,—and Thy steadfast seraphim !

101.

" All praise be Thine—not ours—for constancy
Of service.   Left, unguided, uninspired,
Unaided, unimpelled, O Lord, by Thee,
The brightness even of those Thou hast attired
With crowns of splendour, near Thee, had expired
In darkest wanderings of the will : the speed
With which we haste to go, with fervour fired,
Afresh, perpetually, on holy deed,
Had sunk to slowness, didst Thou not our fervour feed.

102.

"Thy gladdening smile we feel to be our life ;

And life it gives us now : happy, renewed

Existence, with the will and powers all rife

With zeal for high employ and amplitude

Of service : neither with less zest imbued

For lowliest work—so that we shelter fling

Round Thine own saints who suffer in the feud

With evil,—or bold rebels, humbled, bring

Low at Thy feet in tearful penitence to cling.

103.

" We see the sign of love beneath Thy feet,

That now, with energy renewed, we go

Again on Thy blest errands.   When we meet

Once more around Thy throne in bliss to bow—

Another round of duty done—not slow,

We trust, we shall have proved in zeal for Thine

All-righteous rule.   Go with us, Father, go !—

Or vigour of saint and angel shall decline,

And we shall fail to execute Thy will benign.

104.

" The presence of Thy visible glory, Lord,

We leave ; but let us feel Thee ever near,

Where'er we go, and that Thou dost afford

Us loving aid while, serving in Thy fear,

We do our works of love.   O Father! drear

The spaces of Thy universe would be

Without Thyself.   Blest Father! ever cheer

Thy sons with consciousness that, while they flee,

To do Thy will, Thou still art with them : they with

    Thee!"

105.

Their choral praise was ended ; but my rhyme

Is all unworthy of the theme.   Inane

Were all attempts the choir of that pure clime

Of highest heaven, and their ecstatic strain

Of holiest worship, with the grand refrain,

So oft repeated, of their grateful joy,

To celebrate.   To leave God's high domain

They now prepared, in lower realms employ

To share: to help the good, or evil to destroy.

106.

Bright order still they kept.   Who led the van ?
God's holy Martyrs—with no banner spread,
Or ensign—but they; first, with zeal began
The crystal walls to pass—to join the dread
Encounter, still, with evil : firm their tread
Upon the golden floor !   And, marshalled forth
By resident seraphim of heaven, were led
To the gates the myriad hosts, beside—on earth,
Or other realms of God where first their souls had birth,

107.

To re-enjoy their work for Him—their high
And rapturous toil of love and service blest.
The resident seraphs, and the beasts that cry—
Saying, " Holy, holy, holy!"—and never rest—
The spiritual creatures full of eyes—and drest
In white, the Elders crowned, who, by the sea
All-hyaline, before the Throne, attest
Likewise, perpetually, the sanctity
Of God Almighty—by His loving, high decree,

Remained in heaven—to me, to know 'twas given—

Ever with rapt and holy worship, there :

Within the Lamb's own light, in highest heaven

Remained to praise.
        I heard a voice declare:

" Thou shalt return ! " as I the precincts fair

Of bliss prepared to leave.   A thrill of bliss

Awoke me ; and I, trembling, breathed a prayer :

" Lord ! let me not by sin, or cowardice

In the discharge of duty, the blest guerdon miss

" Of joys ineffable, in Thy glad realm

Of heaven ! Henceforth, through every waking hour

Let me be breathing prayer !   If trouble whelm

My spirit, and dark shapes of evil lour

Upon me—even in the hour and power

Of darkness, Saviour, let me feel Thee near !

Through Thee, let me be more than conqueror

O'er sin, and sloth, and pride, and doubt, and fear ;

And then, Thy voice saying, ' Come up hither ! ' let

    me hear ! "

NOTES TO BOOK I.

[1] Stanza 24.   An allusion to the Hall of Suicide Kings, in Book I. of "The Purgatory of Suicides."

[2] Stanza 26.   "Dear, dear land,"—dying speech of Gaunt, in Shakspere's Richard II.

[3] Stanza 40.   Another allusion to "The Purgatory of Suicides," Book I., Stanza 36.

BOOK II.

COME forth, my Love! Old Winter, harsh and
    frore,

Flees the young vernal sun! Come forth, my Love!

Let us renew sweet childhood's joys once more:

Once more return with merriment to rove

Adown the dear old lanes, through the loved grove,

O'er mead, and marsh, and pasture! Though with
    lithe

And limber steps we can no longer move,

The flowers will laugh around us! Ere Death's
    scythe

Shall reach us, let us share again Spring-pleasures
    blythe!

2.

What say'st thou, Love—"Will there be flowers in
    heaven?"
They should grow there, Love, for thine own sweet sake.
But, while on earth we stay, and flowers are given
To us on earth so lovely that they make
Our hearts rejoice within us, and oft wake
A wonder whether saints in bliss behold
Aught that doth seem more truly to partake
Of rapturous loveliness than flowers unfold
Of loveliness on earth, though only of earth's mould,

3.

Let us go forth, and look into their eyes
Of love, once more!
              Old faces, ever new,
Men would look fondlier on ye, were they wise:
Ye harbour no ingratitude: the view
Of your bright beauty breeds no spite: your hue
And splendour raise no jealousies: content
Is your inheritance, and ye subdue
Aspiring thoughts in man: most eloquent
Is your frail life how briefly mortal life is spent!

4.

How oft your mute but holy chaplainship

Hath led the heart of man to holiest prayer :

Heart prayer : more true than orisons o' the lip !

Still let me seek ye in the freshening air

Of morn ; and as ye ope your eyes so fair,

And look towards heaven,—upward I'll look

With grateful love, and humbly cast my care

On Him who careth for ye, in your nook

Wherein so lowlily ye nestle.   In His Book

5.

I learn He loved ye, when He walked on earth

With lowly men, and taught them that the king

So wealthy and wise was not, with all his girth

Of glorious robes and jewels glistering,

Arrayed like one of ye !—

                Welcome, sweet Spring—

My natal time !—How I could love to live

For ever here, if thou wert garlanding

The earth, alway.   Thanks; rather, let me give

For joys thou giv'st : this life of joy is fugitive !

6.

Come forth, my Love! the sorrel of the wood—
Thy darling tenderling—in mossy shade
Now blossoms, and the bluebell is in bud ;
The primrose waxeth wan, like love-sick maid.
O violet sweet! hath thy rich hue dismayed
Thy pale companion ?—Let's to the brooklet's edge !
See how the turbaned geum hath displayed
Its pride !—Step hither, darling, through the sedge:
'Twill glad thine eyes: I've found the golden saxifrage !

7.

Hark! 'tis the cuckoo : Spring's true harbinger !
We all feel sure 'tis Spring—'tis life renewed—
When that quaint note—quaint, yet beloved—we
    hear !
How wondrous 'twas in childhood !   All unviewed,
The curious voice with ardour we pursued,
Imagining the wood, the vale, the hill
Contained it,—nor desire to run subdued
Easily, though out of breath !   How like our will
To follow fancies that can ne'er the wide soul fill !

8.

List, list again! the stock-dove coos her coy

But fervent love; that lowly minor song

The yellow-hammer sings brings back the joy

Of early years; the linnet perched among

The golden gorse doth tenderly prolong

Old, sweet remembrances; while, overhead,

The soaring lark, in anthems clear and strong,

'Leads back desire to joys that will bestead

The yearning soul most truly while on earth we tread.

9.

But, list again!   How tear the heart away

From earth, while listening to yon flute of gold

The blackbird sweetly plays?   What powerful sway

Hath such rapt music for the soul!   Oh cold,

Relentless Death! how I thy power controlled

Could wish, that I might ever stay on earth

And listen to her music manifold!

What wonder that her music and her mirth

Have such enchantment for a thing of earthly birth?

10.

What tiny woodman's axe rings lightly down
Our path? Lo, yonder to the rotten tree
Clings the green-feathered worker, with his crown
Of burning crimson! With what saucy glee
The bar-winged jay and magpie laugh to see
Their neighbour's toil! Let idlers all deride—
He works in earnest, having found the key
To unlock the insect treasures that there hide:
Well done, fair bird! work on, whether they laugh or
   chide!

11.

Shall we press inward, to the thicket dern,
Where rare Herb Paris springs, and orchids flout
The mystic stranger, 'mid young snake-curled fern?
Hark! in the swamp, how merrily the rout
Of snow-white crowfoots seem to sing and shout:
"We are as fair as lilies!" Many a year,
Loved lilies of the vale! with hope devout,
In vain, I've sought ye, and begin to fear
The music of your fairy bells I shall not hear

12.

As in Lea Wood I heard it, when—a child,

Love-guided by my brave dear mother's hand,

I went to pluck ye, and my mother smiled,

Forgetting her oppressors 'midst the bland

And gladdening smile of Spring. 'Midst yon bright
  band

I soon shall meet her—for, in Christ she died!

Sweet Lord, I thank Thee, that in Thy glad land

No woe or weeping shall the Poor betide:

No more their souls shall ache beneath the scourge of
  Pride!

13.

Away, old sorrows of the heart, away!

How surely do your memories live, though years,

We think, have buried them! But now sweet May

Hath come, this is no time for sorrow's tears.

Let tears flow, rather, from the fount that nears

The fount of sorrow, in the soul : so twin

Is all our nature! on the face that wears

The clouds of sorrow radiant joys soon shine ;

And smiles to tears, soft, whisper—"Lo, we are akin!"

14.

"It is the merry, merry month of May!"—
So sang we in our childhood; and the song
Let us sing cheerily 'mong the flowers so gay!
They are not fallen to sin, or stained with wrong.
O give us of your pureness, happy throng
Of virgin starworts!—your untainted show
Of beauty seems more truly to belong
To bliss, because so near the ground ye blow:
Even fairest flowers seem happiest when they humbly
    grow.

15.

And humble as thy name doth thee betoken,
Lowly ground-ivy, not a cultured flower
Of which we hear words superfine fairspoken,—
Whether in trim parterre or lady's bower,
Or grand conservatory,—holds a dower
Of richer splendour than thy purple dye!
Nor seems the dahlia, in its robes of power,
More beautiful than thy meek fairy eye,
And tinct serene, as of the noon-day summer sky,

16.

Dear speedwell, that so modestly dost cower

Under the hedgerow!   Pilewort, with its sheen

Of gold, and daisy silver-rayed,—the flower

So dear to every child !—with lovelier mien,

Seem to gaze on us from their couch of green

Upon the ground, than if they did look down

From lofty boughs of lordly forest treen.

From lofty things we rather fear a frown,

Than look that smiles by them upon the earth be strown.

17.

What hast thou found ?—the fairy moschatel ?

How fitly did the wise and reverent Swede

"Unglorying" name it! He named all things well—

The lowly interpreter of Nature : freed

From base self-worship, all things did him lead

To enthrone the All-Worshipful, and trace His hand

Of tireless care and wisdom in each weed,

Each winged and creeping thing, proud man hath

banned,

As much as in the beautiful, the gay, the grand.

5

18.

There goes the startled throstle from her nest !

Come, let us seek for it, but not destroy

Or rudely touch its precious treasure, lest

The bird should grieve when she comes back to pry

If all be safe. *Eureka !*—when a boy,

If I had found five eggs so beauteous blue

And speckled, I should have gone wild with joy !

I wish I had found out the value true

Of other pretty things I did so long pursue

19.

Only to find them valueless and void

Of aught to make man happier.   How the eyes,

The ears, the taste, and every sense beside,

Deceive us !—and, when undeceived, what sighs

We heave to be deceived again !   Disguise

It as we may, the winsome world we deem

So false is chiefly our own making.   Lies

Will sparkle as if writ with Truth's own beam

To minds content to rest on hopes that only seem.

20.

Our steps grow weary, Love ! Let us wend home—
Though home we share no longer, as in days
Gone by. Worn pilgrims, through the world we roam,
Calling no cot " our own," kindling no blaze
On our own hearth, bidding a friend who pays
His evening visit " welcome ! " now, no more.
What then ? We know no want: so let us raise
Our thankful hearts unto the Great Bestower :
Life shall be DUTY while it lasts ; 'twill soon be o'er !

21.

My evening task wrought out, once more, when sleep
Imperfectly again had shut out sense
Of outward things—which, evermore, we threap,
Are real and true, while but a fraudulence
Of brain o'er-busy 'tis, or indigence
Of gastric power, that fills the mind with dreams,—
I dreamt again that I had audience
Of martyred souls in converse on high themes :
A company brightly clad with heaven's own glorious
    beams.

22.

The Martyr's names ybore of reverence—names
A false religion teaches men should hold
As mediatorial.　But, I wis, no claims
On earth they made so arrogant and bold ;
And their descant in heaven left all untold
Such fictions of old Priestcraft.　Holy Paul
The persecutor saved—I did behold ;
And with him Peter and James ; apostles all
Of Him who died to save their sinful souls from thrall.

23.

They spake not of the kind of death they died :
Not Paul of his beheading ; nor if on
The self-same day Peter was crucified [1]
Head downwards, in the spiritual Babylon ;
Nor of the sword wherewith the brother of John
Was slain, by murderous Herod, heard I word
Of boasting made by James.　And when, anon,
There met them James, the brother of the Lord,
Surnamed " the Just," he spake not of the old record,

24.

How lawlessly the Pharisaic mob

Hurled him sheer down from off the temple's wing,

And beat his brains out with a fuller's club,[2]

Because full often they had felt the sting

Of his reproofs amid their trafficking

With vice in virtue's name.   No thought of pride

Did to the souls of the Apostles cling,

While speaking of the Past.   It seemed beside

A stream of Paradise, in lowliness, they hied.

25.

Most gratefully they spake of what they owed

To their most loving Lord ; and of the grace

He gave them, while upon the earth they trode,

His saving truth to welcome and embrace ;

And power to war with old affections base,

Within ; and strength and boldness to proclaim,

Alike to Greek and Jew, in every place,

The Gospel of God's Christ ; and His high Name

To enthrone where'er they bore the cross, despising

shame.

26.

And then they spake, in wonder, how such weak

And faulty creatures as on earth they felt

They were, God should have used His truth to speak

And spread so widely through the realms where knelt

Fallen men to brutish idols :—from the belt

Of Libyan sand, and by the pillars named,

Falsely, of Hercules, where the Iberian Kelt

Worshipped the sun ; and all around the famed

Great Mediterranean Sea, 'mong nations haughtily

    claimed

27.

For vassals by the imperial men of Rome,—

To question-loving Athens, Corinth lewd—

Of merchandise and wealth and sin become

The heart of Greece, in her decrepitude ;—

And through the isles o'er the Ægean strewed ;

And in the stately cities of Levant,

And Lesser Asia ; till again were viewed

The prostrate peoples who, with fire and chaunt,

Knelt to the sun, in degradation jubilant !

28.

And then they blessed the holy name of Christ,

That now His truth across the seas was borne

To men in late-found regions; and rejoiced

That Gentile nations whom their sires with scorn

Had looked upon, and treated as forlorn,

Forsaken things of God, were filled with zeal

For Christian truth.   And then they 'gan to mourn,

As happy spirits mourn in heaven, and feel

For brethren who reject blindly their highest weal.

29.

" Oh that our brethren who on earth still boast

Of father Abraham's seed "—were the earnest cries

Of holy Paul—" from grovelling in the dust

Would cease, and strive to win the blessed prize

Of life we share in Jesus' Paradise!

When from their sight will they let fall the scales

Of stubborn prejudice, and exercise

The gift of patient thought, that never fails

To find out truth, when earnestness in men prevails,

30.

"And preference for the truth, whate'er betide
Him that embraceth it?   For God doth aid,
Unknowing to the seeking soul, and guide
Its search for truth.   'Twas thus displayed
Was His large pity, although fierceness swayed
My spirit, and I burned to shed the blood   .
Of Jesus' saints.   His holy eyes pervade
Men's thoughts, marking their yearnings for the good,
And leading them by ways they have not understood."

31.

"Yet, 'twas not patient thought, my brother Paul,
I trow, that saved thee," with fraternal smile
Spake Peter; "rather say 'tis goodness all—
Free, sovereign goodness—that doth choose the vile:
The persecutor, thou—on murder bent, the while:
The faithless, I, who did deny my Lord:
'Tis sovereign goodness that doth reconcile
Fallen men to God."
                    "For ever be adored
That goodness! Thou hast spoken the wiser and better
    word "—

32.

The great apostle of the Gentiles said,

With noble haste of meekness. "We must wait

The Lord's good time. 'Twill surely come. The dead

Shall rise to holy life. God will create

Israel anew. His people's afterstate

Of bliss on earth shall come. Men shall behold

The day when every Jew shall hail God's great

Messiah—Jesus the Nazarene—their old

Rapt seers with joy beheld, and rapturously foretold."

33.

"Yet God," said James, the martyr of that lewd

And cruel king who gave the dancer vain

John Baptist's head for fee, "still lets the feud

Prevail 'tween Jew and Gentile. And the reign

Of Christ on earth seems distant far. The strain

Of triumph for the lowly Jesus swells

Not yet, o'er land and sea. Old Error's chain

Still binds half earth. The dark-skinned heathen sells

His children to the white for gold. Earth's lands are

hells

34.

" Of evil yet, in spite of all God's strife

With men, and Christ's dear suffering, and the zeal

Of His dear saints.   And yet may many a life

Of Christian men be taken by the steel

Of murderers vile who bear the outward seal

And name of Christ.   Or, men may have to burn,

In scores, for Christ's own truth, till nations feel

How bitter is the bondage they have worn

Beneath the Man of Sin : that priest of pride and

    scorn ! "

35.

Thus, while they spake, came other spirits I knew,

By mystic intellection, to belong

To apostolic times : the holy Jew,

Stephen, they stoned to death—that raving throng

Whose clothes Paul held, believing right was wrong,

And truth was falsehood ! Now to him Paul cleaved ;

And Stephen grasped Paul's hand with fervour

    strong—

Seeming to feel the highest triumph achieved

For Christ, since even the persecutor fierce believed.

36.

With Stephen came the martyr in old age,

Brave Polycarp;[3] and Justin,[4] who to Antonine

Addressed apologetic words, the sage

Imperial moralist from fell design

And murderous deed to win unto benign

And tolerant regard towards Christian men,

But failed; and Simeon, of the Saviour's line;[5]

And bold Ignatius,[6]—of so lively ken,

He looked as he would gladly face the lions agen!

37.

"We spake, but now, of earth, and our own race,"

Said James, the brother of the Lord, with look

Of love fixed on the martyr Stephen's face;

" Regard for Abraham's seed must be unshook

Within us, even in heaven. Thou, in the book

Divine, in mortal life, wert deeply skilled,

Nor hath thy yearning soul desire forsook

To know the fulness of the words that filled

Thy heart with hope, yea, oft with joy thy bosom
        thrilled.

38.

"Ages have rolled away since we of earth
Ceased to be habitants ; and Abraham's seed
Still count God's great Messiah of no worth.
They deem He earned the malefactor's meed—
.The scourge, the thorns, the cross, the spear; and feed
Their mean imaginations with a king
That shall be clothed with pomp and power, and
    lead
The conquered heathen of their wealth to bring
To his footstool a world-collected offering.

39.

"Or, wise in grovelling doubt, but fools become
Perforce of their own wisdom, they avow
Their bold belief that wild delirium
Impelled God's seers to utter words of woe
Or rapture, and the kingdom to foreshew
Of His Anointed One.   No Christ—they say—
There hath been, or there shall be.   Of the Foe—
The Antichrist—they swell the battle-array,
Eager as their idolatrous sires for Falsehood's fray !

40.

"Oh say, loved brother, who the holy seers,

And their deep meaning, ponderest still, change not

Thy cherished hopes for Israel into fears?

Shall our own race to faith in Christ be brought

By holy influences unknown, unsought,

In their long stubbornness?"—

               "They shall return

To heart-obedience; and then fully fraught

With willingness to know, their souls shall learn

The truth of Christ, and all their hearts with love shall

    burn

41.

"To Him their erring fathers crucified!"—

With hóly haste, cried Paul; "blindness in part

Hath happened unto Israel, till the tide

Of Christian truth fill every Gentile heart;

And then the Jew shall worship; and, athwart

And thorough universal earth shall rise,

Alike from polished Frank and Ethiop swart,

The hymn of gladness that shall pierce the skies,

And draw even angels down to list men's harmonies!"

42.

The face of Paul glowed with a holy light ;

But Stephen's countenance with a brightness shone

Transcendent as the sun above the night

When earth is roofed with stars, as he made known

How strong his confidence in God had grown,

And God's great purpose to His prophets told,

In ancient times, and o'er the record strown

Of Holy Writ, in syllables of gold,

That did to faithful minds their meaning bright unfold.

43.

"To Zion shall the Redeemer come," he sung ;

"And Jacob's late-born sons their sin shall leave ;

And God with fire of praise shall touch their tongue,

When they at length His holy truth perceive.

And they no more His Holy Spirit shall grieve,

Nor shall their children, to the latest hour

Men shall exist on earth. Israel shall cleave

Unto the covenant-keeping God, their tower

Of strength; and hallow His high Name for evermore!

44.

" Zion shall rise and shine, and know her light

Is come, and that the glory of the Lord

Hath risen upon her darkness ; and the sight

Shall draw the grateful Gentiles toward

God's house of glory that shall be restored

On David's hill ; and kings shall haste to own

The King of kings, in David's city adored ;

And Midian, Ephah, and Sheba shall cast down

The golden burthens of their camels before His throne.

45.

" All Israel's sons shall gather from afar,

And flow together, first with fear—with joy,

Full soon—for men from under every star

The abundance of the sea shall bring, and cloy

Jerusalem with good.   It shall upbuoy

The Gentile heart with gladness to join hand

In hand with Abraham's sons, while all employ

Their tongues to swell Christ's triumph, in one band

Of holy brotherhood out-gathered from every land.

46.

" I see, with eyes of faith, the flying cloud

That, like a flock of doves, in joy return

Unto their windows!   I behold the crowd

Of nations who our race beheld with scorn,—

And long did contumeliously spurn

And bruise,—now haste to bring the exiles home!

Lo ! Judah's children from their long sojourn

Among the isles, in ships of Tarshish come !—

How shall the ruined narrow city find them room ?

47.

" The sons of strangers shall her walls extend

O'er neighbouring hills, and kings, the work shall aid ;-

For now the days of God's just wrath shall end,

And His sweet favour and mercy be displayed :

Jerusalem in joy shall be arrayed ;

And through her gates, that shall continually

Be open, day and night, the new Crusade—

The host of love and peace—in holy glee

Shall crowd, from every shore washed by the surging

    sea !

48.

" Her, all the haughty kingdoms of the earth
Shall serve, or perish.   Even the fierce and high
Who brought her sorrow, now shall bring her mirth:
Yea, bending lowly, they shall come and lie
Repentant at her feet.   And all shall vie
In zeal to pile with votive wealth the floor
Of God's new sanctuary : for beautify
His place on Zion He will again : no more
To be cast down by proudest king or conqueror !

49.

" Though once forsaken, and her name with hate
Rehearsed, the Zion of the Holy One
With plenty and with joy shall be elate.
The Mighty One of Jacob shall make known
That He, the Lord, Her Saviour, for His own
Hath taken her ; and men no more shall raise
The cry of violence in her streets, or groan
Of sorrow in her homes, through countless days :
For they shall call her walls Salvation—her gates Praise!

6

50.

" Her sun shall never more go down, or moon

Withdraw its light.   Her everlasting light

The Lord Himself shall be: no clouded noon

Of mourning she shall know, no cheerless night.

Of sorrow: Righteousness shall rule with bright

And smiling sovereignty o'er all God's realm:

The branch of His own planting, in His sight

Shall flourish; and the weak the strong o'erwhelm;

And glory sit on Israel's spiritual warrior helm !

51.

" The Lord will hasten it, in His own time !"—

He sang, with lips touched with a coal of fire

From the same altar, the prophetic rhyme   ·

Of him who struck with noblest hand the lyre

Of all that God-inspired and matchless quire

Who woke the echoes of each rocky dell

Through Judah's land, what time the armies dire

Of proud Assyria threatening came, but fell

By the destroying angel's hand,—without a knell,—

52.

Dead corpses all,—found in the early morn ;

And Sénnachérib fierce to Nineveh fled,

And died by slaughterous hands of children born

From his own loins :—while, as one from the dead

New risen, meek Hezekiah raisèd his head,

And he, and all Jerusalem, wondering, knew

How soon from threats that fill the heart with dread

God can deliver men—how soon subdue

His people's foes, that murderously their souls pursue.

53.

Isaiah's lofty song the martyr sang ;

And all sang with him, as they caught the strain ;

While, as they sang, loud heavenly echoes rang

Of elder songsters making sweet refrain.

And, forthwith, these appeared—a stately train

Of reverend forms—the minstrel leading them—

Isaiah's self : he who was sawn in twain [7]

In his old age, by one the diadem

Vho stained, of Judah : impious fruit of pious stem :

54.

Idolatrous Manasseh, who became

A penitent in trouble, and made prayer

To God, who raised him from his prisoned shame,

And set him on his throne again—the rare

And precious fact in history to make fair

For all men's gaze, through time—that kings may keep

A promise made in trouble and despair,—

Though, trouble past, they usually hold cheap

Even oaths, and lightly law, most lawlessly, o'erleap.

55.

The primal martyr, Abel, next, I knew:

The son whom our first mother wept to see

Of life bereft; and whom his brother slew—

Her first-born son. A martyr, sure, was he—

The first of men that died ! By enmity

Of sin to holiness the victim fell';

And, through all years, bad men have raged to be

Convicted of their ill by men who well

Have lived; and sought, in blood, the hated good to

quell.

56.

The son of Barachiah, slain between

The temple and the altar,[8] eke, I saw,—

With unnamed prophets whom the kings obscene

Of Judah and Israel slew, to gorge the maw

Of wickedness with righteous blood : God's law

Despising, and His vengeance drawing down—

At length—when that great prophecy with awe

The twelve disciples heard their Lord make known

Was full; and temple and altar were alike o'erthrown.

57.

Last of the train came he who was the last,

Of God's high messengers that went before

His Christ : he who proclaimed, as with the blast

Of a shrill trumpet, on old Jordan's shore—

" I am the voice of one foretold of yore—

The herald crying in the wilderness—

Prepare the way of the Lord !"   Aspect he wore,

Elijah-like, of courage questionless,

That seemed his brethren with a sense of awe to

impress.

58.

And thus he spake : " With rapture, still on earth,

Blest prophet, by believing men thy song

Is sung ; while unbelievers turn to mirth

Thy bright foretellings, saying—Declare how long

Shall Israel dwell in banishment, and wrong

Receive from nations who Isaiah's God

Adore—Isaiah's Christ with fervour strong

Profess to love? When shall the heavens be bowed,

And Christ descend on Olivet,—upon the cloud—

59.

" They said they saw receive Him—the eleven

Who gazed so steadfastly upon the bright

Shekinah which upbore Him into heaven,

His native seat,—while, by them, two in white,—

The attendant angels,—pointed to the sight,

Saying—This same Jesus shall again descend,

Clothed in like manner with the cloud of light,

As ye have seen Him go ? When shall the end

Of this world's kingdom be? Show us what sign

portend

60.

"The second coming of the Christ foretold

By fablers, and by doting men believed?

Where doth the wolf lie down within the fold

With the young lamb, in peace? Who hath perceived

The cow, no longer of her calf bereaved

By the grim bear, feed with him, while their young

Lie down together? What child hath achieved

The fearless feat to dare the forky tongue

O' the cockatrice, and play upon its den unstung?

61.

" We see no signs that your famed Prince of Peace

Shall come, and o'er the happy nations reign.

The wolf—the Christian shepherd—yet doth fleece

The sheep ; the royal lion and leopard drain

The life's blood of the labouring ox : in vain

We look for serpents that with children play,

And harm them not : knaves still the simple swain

Entrap and rob. Thus, ages pass away—

If Christ will come, why doth He thus delay?

62.

" So, in old time, the Pharisee and scribe,

Who listened to the Saviour's warning word,

Denied His truth, with scoff, and jeer, and gibe,

And, voluntarily blind, His claims ignored.

But, on their children was the vengeance poured

That Christ foretold. And yet will God, blest seer!

Thy prophecies fulfil.   Again the Lord

Will come in judgment ; but will first appear

In mercy. They who wait for Him discern Him near!"

63.

Although in Paradise, the son of Eve,

With looks and words of mingled sorrow and love,

Began : " The first of martyred men must grieve

For memory of that brother who first strove

Against his brother.   For the curse hath clove—

The curse of murder—to our sinful race,

Since first the spirit of evil did Cain move

To shed his brother's blood : no resting-place

The wanderer found : he ever saw the fancied face

64.

"Of the avenger.   And the murderer still

Doth tremble at the sound o' the fallen leaf—

And yet men murder !—yet, with rebel will,

Men wander from all good, and spend their brief

Sojourn on earth in filling it with grief!

I would the day were come, O Prophet sweet,

When how to bless each other shall be chief

Of men's desires and thoughts—when men shall
   greet

Each other with true loving hearts where'er they meet!

65.

"I would thy glorious vision of the joy

And love and peace that men on earth shall feel,—

The works of love and peace that shall employ

Their hearts and hands,—the Present would reveal.

The Past hath wounds that no regrets can heal ;

And, in the Future, until earth become

A world of loving men who for 'the weal

Of others toil unselfishly,—its gloom

Brings sorrow to my soul, even in this blissful home !

66.

"Bear with me lovingly, dear saints of God !

Ye scarce can feel as I feel.   When I came

A stranger here, where none but angels trod

This Paradise of blessedness ;—where name

Of Man itself was new ;—not without shame

And awe I witnessed how, with piercing eyes,

The angels wondered, when from fiery flame

And axe, and other deaths of hideous guise,

Truth's victims crowded hither, slain by Men of Lies !

67.

"And, through the long, long ages, still arrives

The host of martyred men from earth.   The hate—

The deadly hate—of evil men survives

For good men—oh, how long!   I watch and wait,

But see not that their rage for murder doth abate.

O Lord, how long——"

     "O gentle son of Eve ! "

Isaiah gently spake : " doth not the Great,

The High and Lofty One wait also ?   Grieve

His essential Love it must—doth not thy soul believe—

68.

" That still His saints fall victims to the rage

Of murderous brothers who are mad with sin ?—

Could He not end them ?—or, their wrath assuage ?

But why, or wherefore, did their being begin ?

God is all-wise : His work is not akin

To man's : abortive oft.   And, if away

God took man's freedom, none reward could win

Who served God ; and man's worship would convey

No praise unto God's ear, though it should last for aye.

69.

" Thy gentle soul, O Abel, doth with love—

With pitying love—for suffering man, run o'er.

But, doth not God's forbearance larger prove

His love and pity—since He wields His power,

Not to crush sinners ; but, His grace to shower

Upon their hearts, to soften them, and bring

Their wills towards good : although the noble dower

Of freedom that He gave, He will not wring

From man or angel : His own work disparaging.

70.

"We may not wish that the All-wise had laid

The vast foundations of His universe

According to our wisdom ; or had made

Intelligent creatures whom He did coerce

To keep His law, whom sin could not amerce

With suffering. What our Holy God hath done

Is done in goodness, as in wisdom. 'Sperse

Thy sorrow with the thought, O gentle one !

O' the joys of men and angels since their being begun."

71.

" I do adore His wisdom, and confess

His goodness infinite," meekly replied

The son of Eve ; "my thought is languageless

When I would sum the good that is allied

Even with suffering. Yet again the tide

Of grief will swell, amid the joys of heaven,

When I bethink me how the earth is dyed

With blood of God's dear saints. From it long riven,

To lingering love of its old home the soul is given."

72.

"Sweet patriarchal spirit, and brethren dear!

I speak with diffidence, where elders tell

Their thoughts"—said Justin, the philosopher—

"Thoughts of deep mysteries that often dwell

In human hearts untold, until they swell

To bursting : for, men bind each other down

With chains that cause the spirit to rebel—

Forbidding men to think—until men moan,

And wish they never had the gift of thinking known.

73.

"We ever deemed it past man's finding out

Why God had made a universe where death

And sin and suffering could be found—a doubt

To render possible, or shake devoutest faith

That God is what the holy volume saith

He is—the High and Lofty One, the True

And Holy and Good and Loving One, that hath

Been ever, and that ever shall be. But the clue

Of subtler, simpler thought we reach in this the new

74.

" And sinless habitation of the soul—
Wherein her powers are strengthened, and her gaze
Is purged from fleshly films. God hath made all—
We now discern, surrounded with the blaze
Of His perfections—purposely to raise
Within His creatures perfect loving trust
In His unselfishness. In all their ways
Of lauding Him, the children of the dust
Fall short—unnaming that great attribute august !

75.

" It had been selfishness had He but made
A lifeless universe—however wise
Its mechanism and motions had displayed
His mind to be—or beauty of the guise
Of things, Him beautiful that did devise
Their forms and hues, had proven. But one Mind—
His own—the Awful One's—to know or prize
The wisdom and the beauty ! How unkind
Were such Creator in His awfulness enshrined !

" To store His glorious universe with life
God's blest unselfishness His essence moved ;
And thus all worlds with living things are rife.
But, gift of life alone had not Him proved
Unselfish. Living things it Him behooved
To bless—to make them worthy of His hand.
For, if no creature could have known or loved,
Have thought or felt—as well, a barren strand,
Or lifeless ocean, God eternally had planned !

77.

"God were not blest could He not love and feel
As well as know. Vain sages of the East
Affirm their Brahm, the highest, hath perfect weal
Because he is emotionless—divest
Of feeling—joy or grief ; and in such rest—
Such blank quiescence—centres perfect bliss !
But God's word leaves us to no barren quest
About Himself—no cold hypothesis :
It tells us that He hates the sinner's ways amiss,

78.

"But loves the righteous; that He hath great joy
When sinners turn and leave their sinful way,
And seek their Father's house; but that the alloy
Of grief is His when His own people stray
From His sweet service.   If unwise men say—
Can, then, the Unchangeable rejoice or grieve,
And still be perfect?   Yea, we answer, yea:
Unchangeable holiness, His saints believe,
Is His; and higher perfectness none can conceive.

79.

"God's happiness is perfect, not because
He is almighty, or all-wise, or fills
Infinity, or gives all life by laws
Himself supports.   But perfect happiness thrills
His holy essence; since He ever wills
And does that which is holy, perfectly.
Just ire, grief, love—emotions—are not ills
To perfect holiness.   No change shall be
In God's all-perfect bliss throughout eternity.

80.

"And from eternity hath been no change
In His all-perfect bliss, though He hath seen
Men's wickedness, and grieved. Grief was not strange
To God's omniscience.   His creation teen,
He knew, must bring to Him, amid the sheen
Of His all-glorious perfectness—for free
If His creation were, though strong, or keen
In intellect, yet they must ever be
Subject to imperfection, as He did foresee,—

81.

"And though foreseeing, chose to make them free,
And chose to grieve and suffer, that He might
Have creatures in His universe to be
Recipients of His bounty, and delight
Might take in blessing them, and oft requite
With tenderness their base ingratitude,
And follow them in their wanderings from the right—
Leaving it hard for sinful ears to exclude
His call of love with which He hath their souls pur-
sued."

82.

He ceased; not as if all his thoughtful theme
Were uttered, but himself with measurement
Meting of lowliness: nor with esteem
And reverence for God's elder saints unblent
Seemed his demeanour.   Praise, awhile, upsent
The Martyr-host, in silence, with devout
Rapt feeling: silence deep: more eloquent
Than words—for through each visage beamed the
　　thought
Of grateful love with which their wondering souls were
　　fraught.

83.

"Thy words are sooth, my brother," holy Paul
Thus earnestly the silence broke: "for Love
Alone is pure Unselfishness; and all
Our best conceptions, when on earth we strove
To express God's nature, did but feeble prove
Compared with that one sentence of His word—
That God is Love.   The proof is brightly wove
In every sentence of that vast record
The archangels keep of all they know the Sovran Lord

84.

"Hath done, since they primeval light first saw;

And, unto man, the proof is best revealed

In God's best gift of His dear Son, from woe

To save our sinful race. How oft this field

Of thought we visit !—and it still doth yield

Fresh riches, and will ever ; for, again

And oft, this theme will charm us, till unsealed

Is every prophecy, and Christ's great reign

Makes unto men and angels God's great meaning

    plain ! "

85.

A hand of golden light appeared aloft !

The signal seemed to all familiar, for

Upward all glanced, and then around with soft

Benignant smile upon each other :—store

Of love congratulant within the core

Of every heart fraternal beaming bright

Upon their faces, while they left the shore

Of that sweet stream with flowers so richly dight

I dreamt I saw, at first, with new-born spiritual sight.

86.

Obedient to the sign, with lively pace

They trod the plain, till they the hills could climb,

And spoke with rapture of the errands of grace

From which they had returned, in lands of crime

And error that they once, in olden time,

Had known and loved. The martyred prophets said

Old Jordan's banks were fair as in their prime,

But o'er the land the stones of ruin spread

Scarce shewed what glories had belonged unto the
dead.

87.

And when sweet Olivet, and their loved lake,

Gennesaret, the Apostles saw, they told

How burnt within their hearts the words He spake

To them—the Lowly One—in days of old,

As if they heard His voice, and did behold

His meek form still.   And then Jerusalem

They named with words that shewed above all gold

They priced her dust, and thought her still the gem

Of all the earth, though shorn of her old diadem.

88.

But Polycarp spake sadly : " Light hath waned

In Smyrna and our Asian churches, where

It once burned purely. Long hath Falsehood reigned,

Boasting her crescent, in those regions fair.

And, though a few are found not loath to share

Christ's shame, or own His cross,—dark errors blind

Them till their good and ill seem but to bear

A semblance to the grace and beauty shrined

In marbled ruin, which upon that shore men find."

89.

" And Antioch—the beautiful—the great ! "

Said bold Ignatius, " where our faith first found

A name—what marks her now ?   How desolate

And silent are the spaces where the ground

Oft shook with feet of crowds—the air with sound

Of festive shouts was filled "—

                    " Yet, within cell

Monastic, in those lands," said Simeon, " bound

With fetters of the soul, although men dwell,

Sometimes they burst their bondage, we can gladly tell.

90.

" Bethink ye both, my brethren, of the poor
Weak trembler with old age we lately hied
To comfort, at behest Divine, and found the lore
Of Christ his soul had sweetly learned, and tried
To enlighten others.   And he joyous died,
For some had listened to his words with joy,
And learnt to love, in truth, the Crucified.—
O let the bliss we reap from such employ,
Revisiting old earth, all sad regrets destroy!"

91.

But now to climb the mountains ever green
Began the Martyrs.   All, with one consent,
Well-ordered step and timely march were seen
To keep, with bands that up before them went,
Or followed after; and right soon were blent
The myriad voices of the Martyr-throng
In choral triumph.   Voice mellifluent
One raised, at call of them who did belong
Unto the Martyr-host: thus Stephen led the holy song:

92.

"Glory to Thee, the covenant-keeping God!

Who didst our fathers in Thy goodness lead

Back to Thy way, when oft they wandering trod

The path of error, yea, pursued with greed

The rebel road, although for holy seed

Thou hadst them chosen ; and didst from ruin save

Them oft, and them with heavenly manna feed,—

Yea, didst for their deliverance cleave the wave

In which their foes, o'erwhelmed, soon found a watery

    grave !

93.

"O Holy One of Israel ! hear the cry

Our longing hearts now send up to Thine ear !

Our race—the race of Abraham—soon bring nigh

To own Thy great Messiah, from their drear

And cheerless unbelief !   O Lord, bring near

Our brethren, whom to love we cannot cease—

Feeling Thy love, and knowing they are dear

Unto Thine heart, and that it will increase

The bliss of saints to see the wanderers seek Thy peace.

94.

"Lord! bring the wanderers back! Remove the veil
From off the heart of Israel!   Lord, make bare
Thy holy arm of might !   They cannot fail—
Thy holy promises : Thou didst declare
The race of Abraham should for ever share
Thy smile ; and Thou wilt yet their hearts dispose
To love Thee.   Hasten, Lord, the time ! The prayer
Of all Thy grateful saints regard : disclose
The morn when rays of love shall subdue all Thy foes!"

95.

The song went on—the song of love and praise,
And prayer, and zeal for others' bliss.   But now
The inward beckoning came that their glad lays,
For me, must end : unto the mountains' brow
I mote not climb ; but on the earth below
Must longer toil.

　　　　　　　I woke, with thankful mind
That God had given me pleasant life to know
On earth : a life He stores with bounties kind,
And heartfelt joy that dreary doubt is left behind.

NOTES TO BOOK II.

[1] Stanza 23. PETER'S crucifixion, with the head downwards, on the same day as Paul's martyrdom.—*Eusebius, Jerome, Hegesippus, Chrysostom, Prudentius,* etc., etc.

[2] Stanza 24. Death of JAMES "the JUST."—*Eusebius,* Book II., c. 1, and c. 23.

[3] Stanza 36. POLYCARP. For his martyrdom see the Circular Epistle of the Church of Smyrna, in Archbishop Wake's Epistles of the Apostolic Fathers. Also *Eusebius,* Book IV., c. 15.

[4] Stanza 36. JUSTIN MARTYR, the Philosopher. See *Eusebius,* Book IV., c. 16.

[5] Stanza 36. SIMEON, the relative of our Lord. For his martyrdom see also *Eusebius,* Book III., c. 32.

[6] Stanza 36. IGNATIUS. For the authorities respecting his martyrdom see Archbishop Wake's Epistles of the Apostolic Fathers.

[7] Stanza 53. ISAIAH. The account of his martyrdom is derived from a Rabbinical legend; but many commentators accept it, believing that it is referred to in Hebrews xi. 37.

[8] Stanza 56. "ZACHARIAS, son of BARACHIAS, whom ye slew between the temple and the altar."—Matt. xxiii. 35.

BOOK III.

1.

I LOOK, once more, upon the awful sea!

I may not sing of it as lordly Childe—

Albeit with heart-throes—sang exultantly,

As of a steed that under its exiled

And haughty rider bounded with a wild

Feeling of kindred scorn and pride.   His fame

Was glorious in my boyhood ; but 'tis soiled,

They tell me, now.   Oh, can it be that shame

Shall his bright memory hide who bears that laurelled

    name!

2.

I gaze, once more, upon the awful sea—

Not with exultant, but with wondering thought,

And humbled feeling.   'Midst eternity

And boundlessness yon tiny white-sailed yacht,

In the far-off horizon, seems to float!

The wide-spread, silent moor, the tallest hills,

Breed no such thinking in me, awe, and doubt,

As this strange sense, all-undefined, that thrills

My bosom while the measureless sea my vision
    fills.

3.

What *is* Existence?—what Eternity?

What lies beyond our outer life?   Thy waves,

For ever restless, change—O living Sea!—

And our own breathing forms,—the dead, in
    graves,—

Change, ever!   Thy vast waters,—whether raves

The tempest, or the weary winds find sleep,

As poets sing, within thy neighbouring caves,—

The pulse of language with their motion keep,

And seem, like us, to shout and whisper, laugh and
    weep!

4.

Thy waters are not dead.   They truly live :

More truly than the forms that in thee dwell.

These die ; but thou dost still live on, and give

Thy outspread hands, when thy proud billows swell,

Unto the toiling sun, that ye may quell

Death's triumphs ever, and all Life renew.

Your progeny, the clouds and showers, dispel

Earth's barrenness.   And thus, all Life seems due,

On earth—O glorious ministers of God !—to you.

5.

Many-voiced Sea—as the melodious One

Did name thee, in the days of old—

It is a luxury, 'neath the summer's sun,

,To loiter on this Cumbrian shore, and hold

Communion with thy voices manifold.

Scarce louder than the murmuring bee the sound

Seems, now I sit upon this beach sweet-knolled

With thyme, and where the rock-rose doth abound,

And crimson cranesbills clothe with beauty the rough

ground.

6.

And now the air doth tremble 'neath high noon,

And Languor reigns,—how, with thy simple lay,—

Which hath to me, from boyhood, been a boon,

And purest joys brings back to mind, alway,—

Thou, darling yellowhammer, seem'st to play

A witching treble to the waters' bass,—

While other birds are silent : even the gay

And tireless lark seeks now a resting-place,

And hides, beside his mate, among the tall ripe grass.

7.

Sweet thoughts of pleasures past, thy soothing lull,

O Sea, calls up to memory ; but thy shore,

To-morrow, may be strown with mast and hull

Of many a goodly ship, and mind me more

Of my own wrecks of purpose, and the poor

Fruition of endeavour to achieve

Great aims.   'Tis vain such failures to deplore,

Now I am near life's close ; but still will grieve

The soul, though 'tis too late life's failures to retrieve.

8.

Shall I behold thy waves when I have sailed

O'er this life's sea ?   I shall live on, when Death

Hath claimed my clay—his portion.   But unveiled

Is still the Future—the Eternal.   Breath

And pulse I cannot have when its frail sheath

The spirit quits; but still the soul may gaze

Upon thy restless waves, as oft she fleeth

To do God's high behests,—and, without daze,

May, look, O glorious Sun, upon thy gladdening blaze.

9.

Shall after-life be indolence ?   Each thing

Living on earth, whether it will or nill,

The eternal purpose of the Eternal King

Doth most industriously and well fulfil,

Through every change—as thou dost, changing still,

Vast Sea, and still subserving in thy change

The ends of Him who holds thee by His will.

Surely, if franchised souls to some dull range

Were doomed, to God's known ways it were unlikeness

    strange !

10.

Boundless as thy path seems to be, shall mine

Be, in the Future? Yet, how shrinks the soul

At thoughts of boundlessness! What! no confine—

No shore—but on, for ever;—and no goal—

No end! Space still beginning, and the roll

Of days grown dateless, numberless! And shall

This Self, that—like a prisoner on parole,

When It adventures forth to think, a thrall

Soon feels Itself, and hastens back to its poor cloisteral,

11.

Dim-lighted home of flesh, affrighted at

The shapes of mystery It meets—soon quit the gloom

And glimmer of this earth, and try a state

Of veritable existence, in the womb

Of vastness all-illimitable, become

An unclothed spirit, and yet clothed upon

With immortality,—fearless to roam

Through realms of life and realms of thought unknown,—

And still, for ever, feel Its journey scarce begun?

12.

The soul within her prison-house of clay

Shrinks back at thought of such strange life unknown,

As if too perilous it were to stray

Through the wide universe of God alone—

Or, unconsorted, in some planet-zone

That girdles round some far-off solar fire,

With essences that large of ken have grown,

By myriad years of thought, yet never tire

To think and search ; but ever pant for wisdom higher.

13.

Alone, upon the pathless sea, rides yet

The tiny white-sailed yacht.   Since height

Of noon no bark, no shallop, or corvette,

No humble fisher's boat, hath come in sight :

Still lonelily she floats, with sail so white—

Far off—so that no help could landsmen lend,

Were skies to change, and storms to come, with night.

But, God is there !   No storm the ship can rend,

Unless,—His mandate given!—His ministers descend.

14.

So God will be with my frail bark, and thine,

Frail brother, when the unknown seas we sail

Of unknown after-life. The Eye Divine

Is on us here, in earthly calm or gale;

And on each soul that lives beyond the veil

Unrent—each dweller in eternity;

The Hand Divine supports alike all frail

Existences in heaven and earth that be—

For frail were even the archangels, Sovran, without Thee!

15.

Why should I shrink and fear, while I can lean

On the Eternal One? Yet, how I dread

The "inevitable hour"! Some, with serene

Indifference, of the grave as of a bed

Of rest, tell us, they dream—nay, they would wed

Annihilation gladly; while the best

And holiest I have known on earth have said

They had no fear, but longed to reach the rest

That for the people of God remaineth, with the Blest.

16.

With a glad heart I tell—the phantom foul

That threatened *Nothingness,* to terrify

And fill with agony my doubting soul

Hath ceased.   But still—*What can it be to die?*

That thought appalls me. Though with strengthened

    eye

I look triumphantly beyond the grave,

And feel my trustful spirit can rely

On Him who strong, for ever, is to save—

Yet, on Death's self I cannot look with challenge brave.—

17.

The filmy cloud I saw arise, but now,

Hath spread along the sky—a dark portent

That storm is near.   So some slight signal, slow

Or swift, may warn me when my soul now blent

With flesh must leave it. May Death's storm be spent

Quickly, O Blessed Father ! if Thy will

It be,—or, rather, let the veil be rent

All in a moment, while I seek to fill

My daily task,—that so I, with ecstatic thrill,

18.

May pass from mortal to immortal life.

Nay !—let me breathe no prayer so full of fear

And selfishness !   Up, to the battle's strife,

Once more ! until the Master's voice shall cheer

Me, when—the mortal victory won—I hear

Him say, "Well done, thou good and faithful one,

Enter into my joy, my servant dear !"—

Lord, let me fight until the battle's done—

Nor ever wish for rest until the battle's won !

19.

My nightly task—the task of Duty—claims,

Again, my heart and mind : a task now hard—

Nay, harder than he knows, who 'mid fierce flames

Moulds melted metal; or, with body marred

And crampt-up limbs, from sun and daylight barred,

Hews at the coal-seam ; or, whose mighty blows

Ring loud upon the anvil.   Small regard

The peasant lends me !   "Why for him unclose

The bar to knowledge ? want of it he hardly knows ;

20.

"And why disturb him ? "—do ye ask, in scorn,

Or kindly ?—" Leave him to his vulgar toil

And vulgar pleasures.   Teach him not to spurn

The lot of ignorance, and seek the broil

Of thought, lest he encounter the dread foil

To deeper thought all thinkers surely find."—

I dare not join a project that would spoil

My brother-man, whom God hath given a mind

That may be nobly taught, and cultured, and refined.

21.

It cannot be God's purpose that the soul

He meant to live for ever should be left

Untaught, and Man become a larger mole

To burrow in the earth, of light bereft,

Or crawl upon it like the reptile eft,

Unknowing of his heavenly destiny.

They practised on Man's freedom a fell theft

Who praised blind Ignorance, and said that she

Was Mother of Devotion.   Set Man fully free—

22.

Free from the bonds of ignorance and control

Of priests—free from the shackles of his pride

And low self-worship.   Let him know the whole

Of Truth that hath been found, and do not hide

The fact that more Man knows not.   He will chide

Himself, most healthfully, and gladly flee

From error, when himself thus dignified

He fully feels with his own sovereignty

Of soul, as freeborn Man.   O set Man fully free!

23.

And yet, though Knowledge be a precious boon

For Man, he who the task doth undertake

To teach men how to think, no mean poltroon

Must be in courage ; nor, in weakness quake

At proud men's anger ; nor, his task forsake

For others' coldness or dull sloth.   To say

And do as others, nor with boldness break

From tyrant custom, or the gilded way

Of fashion, marks the million : only units stray

24.

In paths of independence, and assert

Their native dignity of Man.   And sloth

Seems rest so needful to poor men upgirt

For out-door labour through the day, it doth

Give pain to one, more than their ways uncouth,

To rouse them with hard messages of right

And wrong.   How, if they sleep, can one be wroth ?

In sooth, he ventures on a work of might

Who strives to keep a weary ploughman wake at

 night.—

25.

My task is done once more : the hour hath passed

More pleasantly than I foreboded.   Yet,

What drudgery 'tis to talk to looks aghast

With helpless wonder ; or that seem to fret

With haste to leave you ; or to figures set

As stark asleep as if nought but the loud

Last trump could consciousness in them beget ;

While others glance around with spirit cowed,

As if they felt like leprous men among the proud !

26.

How different were my labour amid shrewd

Auld Scotland; or th' West Riding, where our keen

Critics-in-fustian sit and inly brood ;

Or, where Northumbrian miners with brave mien

Of kindly frankness earnestly upglean

Your thoughts; or, with the quick-discerning throng

In noble Nottingham ; or, my native scene

Of ancient Leicester ; or, much more, among

Bold Birmingham's array of thinkers stern and strong ;

27.

Or, sceptical Northampton, where the knights

Of Crispin ply the awl, and challenge high

Hurl at old teachers—following all new lights !

Or, grand old Norwich ; or, in Bristol, eye

Of England's west, where good men truly vie

One with another in truly Christian deed ;

Or even 'mid London's shallow foppish fry,—

One might with Truth the mind more easily feed,

Than get dull peasants to such teaching to take heed.

28.

Poor English ploughmen! my very heart doth bleed

For you. Your little children I have passed,

Driven forth in "gangs," to gather stones, or weed,

When scarcely it was daylight, o'er the vast

Wide fen of Lincolnshire,—their eyes upcast

For pity at their driver—the brute tool

Who pushed them on with curses; and "move fast,"

They must, or suffer his hard blows. No school

For the poor ploughman's child! He would be called

    a fool

29.

By his own class, and proud by masters, who

Let his child learn to read God's word instead

Of toiling early and late,—and learning, too,

To swear like the big driver,—and lose dread

For foulest vice, where all restraints are fled,

And sex is rudely mixt. The boy or girl

Brings home a few poor pence each day for bread :

What's all the learning that his head might whirl

With pride, compared with bread, to the poor peasant

    churl ?

30.

Oh, gentlemen of England! in your House
Of power and wisdom, can ye find no heart
To end this wrong so horribly infamous?
Ye could set free the Factory child, and thwart
The chimney-sweeper, who made infants smart
And weep for years; and ye could boldly vote
Twenty gold millions to break up the mart
Of demons who the souls and bodies bought
Of negroes:—Why not seize this evil by the throat?

31.

Landlords! upon *your* land this deed is done.
Doth not the tenant know your word is law?
Forbid the deed, then: tell him he must shun
The sin, and ye will cease the gain to claw,
And lower his rent.—" Idiot! expect to draw
Our teeth, as soon; or, ask to flay the skin
From off our backs! We do not yield one straw!"—
Why, then, right honourables! your sordid sin
I would not share, if your whole rent-roll I could win.

32.

The hour of sleep returns, and still I weigh

The sins of other men.   Upon my own

Black catalogue, with the like keen survey,

I fear, I do not dwell.   Lord, from Thy throne

Look down in mercy still on those who groan

O'er others' sins, and oft forget to judge

Their own!

       When waking consciousness had flown,

My dreaming consciousness returned.   A drudge,

I seemed, at first, among old earthly scenes to trudge.

33.

O'er Croyland Fen, methought, in evening gray,

I toiled, from rural Helpstone,—where poor Clare

Was born,—along the narrow winding way

The monks upraised, in dark old times, with care

And patient labour.   'Twas the desolate and rare

Vision renewed, of forty years gone by,

When—myriad ages past—no rude ploughshare

Had yet disturbed the marsh.   Far as the eye

Could reach there was no tree that grew beneath the

    sky.

34.

A clump of reeds rose, here and there, around
A pool ; and, ghostlike, up the bittern reared
Its head out of the clump, and then to the ground
Sank down, and hid itself, and boomed its weird
And shivering note. But, what most strange appeared
Was that vast moving host of feathered things—
The countless flocks of geese, that homeward steered,
With deafening cackle, and with bleeding wings
Drooped to the ground, while,—heedless of their suffer-
    ings,—

35.

The gooselike gosherd urged them with his staff.
The geese had just been plucked alive,—their quill
To exchange for gold.   The gosherds, with a laugh,
Told me they helped the deed.   But I felt ill,
And hastened on, while overhead the shrill
Curlew, the lapwing, and the heron, flew ;
And, far up in the sky, the soaring, still,
And lordly glede seemed taking surer view
Ere, pouncing, dartlike, down, his screaming prey he
    slew.

36.

I went—the pilgrim of romance—to gaze

On Guthlac's ruined shrine—the hoary pile

Of Croyland ; and the image that pourtrays

King Ethelbald the Mercian, broken and vile,

On that triangular bridge that joined the isle

So sacred to profaner ground, in years

When monks held marish and mere for many a mile.

Darkness was falling as I gazed ; and jeers

From ploughboys that beheld me pained my ticklish

    ears.

37.

So on I passed, to shun the boyish crowd ;

But soon, from weariness, lay down to rest

Upon a grassy hillock, o'er which bowed

A bush in which some late bird kept her nest.

And, as she crooled, I slept.

          Among the Blest—

From sleep within my sleep—again, I seemed

To wake surrounded with the host all drest

In light.   But they whom now I saw—I dreamed—

Were souls I had in mortal life but lightly esteemed.

38.

Stern devotees of mediæval time

They were : brave venturers among savage tribes ;

Daring reprovers, eke, of kingly crime

And priestly sloth ;—who heeded not the gibes

Of their own order ;—nor concealed, for bribes,

The sins of men in purple pomp arrayed,

And crown and sceptre ;—or whom timid scribes

Writ " holy," for they stalked in masquerade

Of cowl and hood, begirt with rope, in cloistered shade.

39.

He whom men call the Apostle of Germany,

I saw—Winfred of Crediton[1]—our Saxon saint,

Named Boniface, when episcopal degree

Was given him by the pope.   In him no taint

Of Romish crime was found, natheless.   Restraint

Or fear he felt not for tiara or crown ;

But, like a Christian true, set forth his plaint

'Gainst papal simony ; and dared to frown

Upon the heathenish sins 'mong prelates shown.

40.

While he hewed down the sacred oak of Thor,

And preached to Hessian and to Frisian throngs

Of barbarous men, and taught them to abhor

Idols and wizards and blood, and sing the songs

Of Christ, the Prince of Peace,—sin that belongs

So often to magnanimous kings he dared

To scan : to Mercian Ethelbald the wrongs

Done to his people wisely he declared,

Until that regal heart to goodness he ensnared.

41.

With Winfred walked his brethren who, of yore,

Were massacred, or slain, by heathen bands—

Eoban, and Adalhere,² and many more—

Meek, self-denying men—men of clean hands,

And minds devout—obeying Christ's commands

From love to Him who first loved them, and spread

O'er Frisic, Hessian, and Bavarian lands

The gospel of their Lord : giving the bread

Of life to perishing men : by no false zeal misled.

42.

Remembering how, on earth, I lightly esteemed
The work of these stern toilers, whom I now
Rightly, by mystic gift of insight, deemed
True martyrs—I beheld, with sudden glow
Of pleasure, drawing near, in goodly row,
A band whom others lightly esteemed, on earth—
Lightly esteemed, and scorned, and trampled low;
But whose meek names I valued at right worth,
And oft felt proud I had with them one tie of birth.

43.

Many of these meek ones died through men whose
    boast—
Oh, of such grievous sin, I blush to tell!—
Was rather than that liberty be lost
Of conscience *for themselves* they would rebel
Till doomsday: yet, like fiercest dogs of hell,
They worried men whose consciences felt fear
Of sin most tenderly; and tortures fell
Of whipping, hunger, and imprisonment drear,
And filthy, and foul, inflicted on God's servants dear.

44

Some of Old England were, and some of New.

Some were the victims of our boasted time

When kingly men in England overthrew

Crowned lawlessness and sanctimonious crime ;

And some died when returned the kingly Mime

To reign and sin right royally.   The rest

Were martyred men and women from that clime

Across the sea where, in the distant West,

Their persecutors found a refuge they deemed blest.

45.

Parnell,[3] I saw, the godly boy that death

Of heartless cruelty who died, i' the wall

Of Colchester's strong castle—with last breath

Entreating they would let the happy thrall

Go home to Christ !   Young Burrough,[4] loved of all

His suffering mates,—with pious Hubberthorn,[5]

And others, who in Newgate drank the gall

Of wrong so meekly ; and Trowell,[6] who was torn

And bruised and beaten, till he ceased on earth to

  mourn.

9

46.

Howgill[7] came on with these—a valiant soul,

A noble warrior for his Lord,—no name

His brethren held more worthy : in the goal

At Appleby he died, with sweet acclaim

Of praise to God that worthy to bear shame

He had been counted, for the Christ he loved !—

With these came hundreds, little known to fame,

Who died in dreary prisons, still unmoved,

By suffering, to desert the faith their souls approved.

47.

New England's victims followed those of Old :

Victims whom barbarous Endicot pursued

With hatred—helped by shepherds of Christ's fold !

Good Mary Dyar,[8] who climbed with fortitude

The gallows' ladder twice.   In mockery lewd

Called down the first time : soon with joy she clomb

Again, to die—saying, sweetly, that she viewed

The Paradise of Christ, beyond the tomb,

Where she had been, in spirit, for days : her heavenly

home !

48.

Next, with unlyric names,[9] joined hand in hand,

Fraternally, came on the faithful sufferers twain

Whose naked bodies, as if they bore the brand

Of vilest felony, or shared the crime of Cain,

Were thrust into the ground, with foul disdain,

Even at the gallows' foot.   Then, Leddra,[10] bright

Hilarious soul, followed—who met death's pain

Crying, "Lord, receive my spirit!"—seeming God's light

To see, with dying eyes : blest Stephen's martyr-sight !

49.

The souls of women, young and old, whom fiends

That dared to claim the name of Christian men

Whipped through New England towns[11]—for they

    were " Friends,"—

A deadly crime !—arrived with these.   And when

These unadorned new-comers met the ken

Of Winfred, and his fellows of the age

Called mediæval, in a flowery glen

Of Paradise, amazed, I saw them wage

A race of love to join—as if their lineage

50.

They knew was one; and though so far apart,
In time and place, they lived on earth, they felt
Their zeal for Christ proclaimed them of one heart.
"Brothers," spake Winfred, "when on earth we dwelt,
And preached to savage Teuton and fierce Kelt,
It scarce was strange that, blind with idol-zeal
And gust for sin,—even while to Christ we knelt,—
They slew us, thinking then to rob and peel
Our tents of gold and silver we could not reveal

51.

" As in our keeping, since no needless load
We carried, cumbered and bowed too much with sin.
But who your deaths and sufferings could forebode—
Your torturous martyrdoms—from your own kin,
Your own dear flesh and blood ?   Nay, that within
The bounds of likelihood might be; but they
Who took your lives professed high discipline
Of self-denial, and could not seek to slay
Ye that your gold and silver might become their prey.

52.

"What was the gain they sought? what earthly good

Could they acquire in slaying ye ?   No hoard

Of wealth ye had, that they should shed your blood

To seize it and possess."

      " Be Christ adored,"

Spake noble Howgill, " though their deed abhorred

We may not, by the nature of the mind,

Forget, we still feel loving pity toward

The men whom bigotry had rendered blind—

Nay, mad—as still it maddens thousands of mankind.

53.

"Dost thou not think, my brother, that as brave

Martyrs for wrong are sometimes found, as for

The right?   I doubt not but that some who drave,

Fiercely, our feeble ones with whipping sore,

From town to town, believed they did no more

Than bounden duty; and if called to bear

Smiting, the rod to death they would have bore

Sooner than name of foul apostate wear,

Or gold and silver as the apostate's guerdon share.

54.

"It was not earthly gain our foes obtained,

Or sought.   Our deaths could not enrich our foes

In any sordid sense.   But still remained

In them the carnal mind that doth oppose

Itself to goodness.   Though, by outward shows

And loud profession, men do oft persuade

Themselves and others that within them glows

True Christian zeal, the proof is soon betrayed

That not one moment its pure fires their hearts pervade.

55.

" How eagerly men praise great earnestness,

Though earnest men are caught by falsehood's bait,

So easily ! Surely, men should laud much less

Quick zeal than slower wisdom.   They who wait,

Patient, at Wisdom's feet, regenerate

Become in spirit, and feel no tyrant will

To fetter the free mind—to emasculate

The soul.   Their victories they win meekly, still

Not seeking to compel, but to persuade the ill :

56.

" To win men over by conviction, clear

And calm, that so the settled mind in ease

May rest, and satisfaction.   Kings no fear

Have of their subjects if their reigning please,

But though meek men may bear kings' wrong decrees,

Their hearts will aye the sceptred wrong disown.

Force never truly reigns : its falseness frees

All men from heart-obedience to the throne :

For force is falseness, even to the simplest clown."

57.

" Ay, force is falseness," said our Saxon saint ;

" And neither force nor falseness masterdom

Can win for Truth.   With us failed false constraint,

When, backed with fancied power from Papal Rome,

We forced the Teuton nations to succumb

To Christ.   In vain we triumphed, as the oak

Of Thor I hewed in pieces.   Awe held dumb

Thor's worshippers to witness the bold stroke ;

But soon their awe was gone—revenge within them

  woke,

58.

"And back to their old homage at the shrine

Of their old Thunder God they went with zeal,

While on ourselves they fell with leonine

And bloody rage.   God did, at length, His seal

Set to His truth, when wiser men the appeal

Made to their moral sense—the meek yet broad

Attack on conscience—which will straight reveal

Its living power in man, though long by fraud

It hath been lulled to slumber, or by force o'erawed.

59.

"I would more wisdom had our earnest toil

Directed. Savage men, like children, might,

We thought, be held by fear or kindly guile,

And taught to fall in reverence at the sight

Of saintly bones or gaudy incensed rite,

As they had fallen before the Sun and Moon,

And Thor and Woden.   Oh, that holy light

Upon our eager minds had clearer shone,

That their dark souls for Christ we might in love

have won!"

60.

" Ye worked according to your light.   And they

By their light—twilight, rather," meekly said

Young Parnell, "now are judged, by Him whose
  sway

Knows neither weakness nor injustice.   Dread

In holiness are His commands : to tread

His courts in heaven, unfit they were : the praise

Of God and of the Lamb who for them bled

They could not sing : but just are all His ways :

Only transgressors of His law its sentence slays.

61.

"None can transgress the law they never knew ;

Therefore, the millions of the heathen live

Their after-life of trial where the view

Of truth and right and wrong God doth them give

In clearness, and His Spirit doth with them strive,

That they may yield their wills to Him, and share

Salvation by His Christ.   Alternative

Of choice they still to exercise may dare.

He saveth none by force : all freely His yoke bear.

62.

" It is our highest bliss to feel we serve

Him freely, who to save us freely came—

To feel that we have no desire to swerve

From holiest service—that we know no aim

Or will but ever, with the holy flame

Of love, to burn towards Him who loving gave

Himself for us.   How worthily His name

Could we extol, if each were but a slave

In act?   It would the worship of high heaven deprave."

63.

" How clumsily men frame their theories

Of right!" Winfred resumed ; " in our dark time,

We strove poor heathen men to christianize,

Believing unbelief a damning crime,

Even when of every Christian truth sublime

They were as ignorant as a child unborn !

Nay, this strange misbelief became the prime

Incentive to our warfare with their scorn

And spite, that we might save them from their fate

   forlorn.

64.

"No gentler motives had our hearts impelled

To venture 'mid their swamps and forests wild,

And dare their savage rage.   Had we not held

Them lost—lost irremediably—exiled

From bliss for ever—we could not have toiled

To martyrdom that we might save their souls.

Thank God! that now the darkness that defiled

Our vision is removed.   No wrong controls

His government : we now discern, wherever rolls

65.

"A world that holds His creatures rational,

There all are judged by perfect equity ;

Not equity by wits fantastical

Apparelled with the seeming drapery

Of fairness, though, in truth, 'tis tyranny

Abhorrent to the sense of right in man

Implanted by his Maker."

                        "We with thee

Adore," spake Leddra, " Him whose marvellous plan

Gives all within the moral and intelligent span

66.

" Of His high rule probation fair and free

And noble.   How we could have feared that ire

Consuming from His holy hand must be

The lot, inevitably, of son and sire

In utter darkness born—that endless fire

Should be their portion who ne'er knew His will,

And therefore could not guiltily conspire

Against His holy government, is still.

Our wonder, and must aye our minds'with wonder fill."

67.

" And yet," after some silence, Adalhere

Spake thoughtfully, "when we beheld how base,

How vile, how shudderingly soul-stained they were

We saw bow down to idols ;—how no trace

Of purity remained in them ;—no place

Within their hearts for aught but lowest lust,

And dark desire, and passionate embrace

Of foul indulgence ;—how could we have trust

That any of their fallen souls would live among the

just ?"

68.

"And in God's holy word," spake Hubberthorn,

With slow and gentle speech, "we were not told

That when men's souls had passed their mortal
    bourne,

There might be to the gaze of some unrolled

A second scene of trial.   If so bold

Our minds had been as to affirm what none

Could truly say, in covenant new or old,

God clearly had revealed,—nor His own Son,—

Had we not trespassed, and beyond our duty run?"

69.

"To be not wise above the written word,"

Meekly, said Mary Dyar, "even when the power

Of God's own Holy Spirit within us stirred,

I always thought was safest.   Yet the hour

Hath been, on earth, when a rich spiritual shower

Of knowledge fell on us, from heaven, that shewed

Us meanings in the word which, heretofore,

We saw not.   May not deeper meanings crowd

The written page not yet revealed unto the proud,

70.

"Who trust in their own reason?"

                               "If the heart

Of truth," young Burrough said, "seek truth from Him

Whose word is truth, will not He truth impart

Unto it in the reading, though with dim

Unlearnèd gaze the page be read?   They trim

The outward lamp in vain, to read and learn,

Whose minds with self-conceit unto the brim

Are filled; and do not for God's own light yearn:

The natural man doth not the things of God discern.

71.

"The Gentiles having not the law, a law

Were to themselves, the apostle briefly wrote :

Briefly, yet fully.   Men may safely draw

Safe inference that the law of conscience ought

To be, and will be, only against them brought

When they are judged."

                             "But, since even conscience fails

To give a truthful light to men untaught

Christ's truth," said elder Howgill; "it curtails

Even good men's hope for men where heathenism prevails.

72.

"Yet, if good men were wise as well, some aid
For reaching deeper truth they might have gained
By patient thought.   In God's own image made—
His moral image—man is not disdained
By his great Maker, though so foully stained
By sin. He doth not cast men off—their being spill—
As some men blunder God hath blundering reigned
In His own universe : not able ill
Or good to make of some, for lack of forming skill !

73.

"God never moral agents made to end
Their being eternally, though they would break
His laws persistently, nor would amend
Their lives at His entreaty ;—nor doth He slake
His vengeance by inflicting on them ache
And torture endless, though they did not know
His law.   He doth poor heathen souls awake
To after-life, and therein doth bestrow
Their path with motives that may lead them from all
     low

74.

"And base preferments into choice of good.

All glory to His holy name! in vain

Christ hath not for the heathen shed His blood,

Millions, in that great spiritual domain

Of Christ—the after-life of men whom chain

Of earthly circumstances bound, enslaved,

And crushed with weight of evil,—now the strain

Of gratitude swell high, that their depraved

And fallen souls Christ hath from endless ruin saved!"

75.

"'Shall not the Judge of all the earth do right?'

I answered oft," spake humble Trowell, "when

Lewd London wits, falsely named erudite,

Mocked at all Christian teaching, in that den

Of beasts London became when citizen

Aped harlot king, in revelry and sneers

At purity and truth.   I answered men,

When any heathen soul 'fore God appears,

That he will find hard measure I can have no fears."

76.

"And that the simplest faith is oft more wise

Than logic subtleties, I make no doubt,"

Again said Winfred; "yet the tears and cries

Of million sufferers in the lands without

Christ's gladdening gospel; and the maddened shout

Of thousands, when beneath the ponderous wheel

Of some huge idol's chariot falls, devout,

The Hindoo suicide; the hideous zeal

O' the heart for sin, which Asian city-crowds reveal;

77.

"The brutal cannibalism and murderous strife

That stain so foully yon sweet South Sea isles;

The dark infanticide; the waste of life

In every vile indulgence that defiles

Both body and soul; the thrift of priestly wiles;

The fattening of the priest, and suffering lean

Of yon poor pilgrim, whom the thought beguiles

That he shall win heaven's bliss by tortures keen,

And crawling vilely on the earth, like things unclean.

78.

"Oh, who can think of Man where yet the sound
Of Christ's dear name was never heard, or where
Men's erring souls reject Him with profound
And stolid ignorance that His yoke to bear
Would make them free,—and not desire to share,
Again, the cheering toil, the suffering sweet
Of Christ's blest heralds who His truth declare
To heathen men ; and teach them to repeat
His name ; and lead them for salvation to His feet ! "

79.

His look was lit with light of pitying love
For souls of men still living in the gall
Of bitterness and bond of sin.   Above,
Around, there seemed to glow, and soon to fall,
A crowning radiance, on the heads of all :—
A token bright that all the Martyr band
That loving spirit sweetly did enthral,
And that with joy, at God's supreme command,
They would return to earth to toil in heathen land !

" Let us rejoice," spake Winfred yet again,

" That now the ministry of love is ours,

As spirit-messengers from God to men ;

That, sometimes, He our essences empowers

To aid with strength the poor weak soul that cowers

At shapes of superstition, and doth pant

For spiritual light where heathen darkness lours

On every side, and nought is ministrant

By tongue, or eye, or ear, unto the heart's deep want.

81

" But lately, Eoban and Adalhere

And I, most gladly hastened to obey

Our gracious Lord's behest, a poor fakeer

To help with spiritual whisperings of the way

Of life.   In old renowned Benares lay

His skeleton form upon an iron bed,

For five long years.   We heard him mourn and pray

To many demon gods with names of dread,

That he to purer light and safety might be led :

82.

" He vowed to arise, and creep on hands and knees

To any idol's shrine, however long

The journey were, in order to appease

The wrath of Seeva, or the vengeance strong

Of Doorga or Kalee ! or, with the thong

Of knotted whip to lash his fleshless frame ;

Or scorch his limbs with fire ; or any wrong

From men receive in silence, even to shame

Of spitting, or contempt outpoured upon his name.

83.

"The light of conscience had grown feeble and dim;

But, as that light is quenchless in the breast

Even of the savage, it still lived in him—

Nay, had become a spectre of unrest

Unto him.   Bodily pain did not molest

His thought ; beneath no suffering did he faint :

With burden of sin alone he was opprest :—

Oh, that he could be cleansed from sin's dark taint!—

He cried, all day, and oft all night, without restraint !

84.

" At last, a sleek-fed Bramin saw him lie,

And proudly bade him rise, since now the coin　　＼

Was spent that he had saved by toil,—whereby

His meagre food was bought,—and said, ' Go, join

The crowd of labouring men, and cease to whine

About the burthen of thy sin, and strive

To bring fanams to Veeshnu's shrine—

For that will better please the gods—to give—

Than thus, in sloth and pain, a loathsome life to live!'

85.

" A crowd of gazers raised him ; but the use

Of joints and thews was hard to be retrieved.

He lived, but paid the forfeit of the abuse

Of life for those five years : unto him cleaved

Palsy and pain, and inwardly he grieved,

Alway, with burthen of his sin weighed down.

The fakeer's iron bed, he still believed,

Nearer true light had brought him ; and a groan

Oft told he wished for leaving it he could atone.

86.

" His misery had grown sore, and all could tell
Around him that Insanity would claim
Him for her victim, if he could not quell
His fiery torture.   So with noisy blame
They urged him to remember the great name
Of Juggernauth, whose worshippers oft found
Relief o' the soul when, sunk in sin and shame,
They had of life been weary.   And, soon bound
To Orissa, toiling on, he reached the festal ground.

87.

" But—not to worship at the shrine obscene !
Twas God's own gracious Providence, we felt,
That led him thither.   One with humble mien,
A Christian teacher, stood, and meekly dealt
Out truth to the crowd.   Full soon the heart did
    melt
Of the poor listener !   'Twas the real relief
His soul so long had sought.   In tears he knelt
At Jesus' feet ; and, like the dying thief,
At once was pardoned, and escaped from all earth's
    grief !

88.

" His joy destroyed his earthly life, but brought

Him joy in heaven !   Oh, many will yet believe

In Jesus' saving truth, they long have taught

The dark Hindoo so patiently. It doth them grieve

That they so little of success achieve—

The lowly teachers who cross ocean wide

To win men's souls for Christ ; but we perceive

Sure signs of coming harvest which shall wide

Wave o'er the world. In grateful patience let us bide!"

89.

" Ever in grateful patience, and in faith,"

Said meek young Parnell ; " God hath also sent

Us to that land where men to shapes of death

And murder bow, while still to them is lent

Such light of conscience that, in discontent

With their own fallen nature, they still crave

To lose sin's burthen, or that life were spent.

And they who yield to Christian teaching brave

Endurance need, while their own sires around them

   rave

90.

"With horrid cursing, and their mothers curse
More horridly the children they have borne ;
And children curse their parents who rehearse
The name of Jesus, as their Saviour. Scorn
And hatred, and a menaced life forlorn,
Or loss of limbs, or death, await on them
Who dare decide for Christ. If some return
To their old vileness, bravely some contemn
All threats of danger, holding precious Truth's bright
　gem.

91.

"They who, in England, mock the enterprise
Of Christian men that preach to the Hindoo,
And, scoffing, ask why he so long defies
Converting power, and is so hard to woo
Unto conviction, and change old for new,
Might cease their gibes if they would mark the tale
Of truthful witnesses. How long the True
Shall thus be martyr to the False, we fail
To know: yet know the True most surely shall prevail.

92.

"It shall prevail as surely as God lives

And giveth life to all that live throughout

His universe.   Himself the assurance gives ;

And He Himself is Truth.   His foes so stout

Shall yield ; the falsely wise shall cease to doubt ;

Barbarian darkness shall behold His light ;

And universal nations join the shout

That God hath come to reign in truth and might :

God and His Christ have come to bring the reign of

    Right ! "

93.

New radiance fell upon that company

Of loving Martyrs while young Parnell spake,

And lit their faces with such heavenly glee

Of holy love, it seemed in me to awake

Deep longing that I could such love partake.

But, now, soft strains of music that I seemed

To recognize began, forthwith, to break

Upon my spiritual ear : the strains I dreamed

I heard before : above, around, they sweetly streamed !

94.

And lo! above the Martyr band appeared
The hand of golden light all quickly saw,
And, seeing, seemed with expectation cheered
Of higher joys.   It did their footsteps draw
Unto the terraced mountains, which, by law
Of their blest spiritual existence, all
Must at appointed seasons, with rapt awe
Ascend, to enter at the trumpet's call
High heaven, and share its worship beatifical.

95.

The mountains ever green, my mind discerned,
Did picture endless life, and endless bliss,
Attained by all who climbed them—all who yearned
To be for ever good : from wrong and vice
Set free—from hate and rage and prejudice
For ever : and their essences imbued
With love and purity : no thought amiss :
No wrong affection : no solicitude—
Except to be in holiness for aye renewed.

The mountains all were terraced, as I knew

Intuitively, that in the realm of rest so bright

No thought of labour might bedim the view

Of God's dear saints *at home.* So light

Was the ascent, it seemed to some a flight

In ether. Yet the sense of order stilled

Each mind, as if the want of it would blight

Their bliss. So up they stepped, as troops well drilled

Step lightly, without toil: each heart with joyaunce

 filled!

And as they 'gan the terraces to climb,

I saw their steps were timed, as in my dream

I saw before: a triumph march sublime

It was; and as they marched they turned the theme

Of their late converse to a tuneful stream

Of choral song; and thus the Martyrs sung :—

"We come, O Lord, to share the quickening beam

Of Thy bright glory with a grateful tongue,

For that Thou hast our hearts with chords of gladness

 strung.

98.

"We laud Thy wondrous love, eternal, vast,

And infinite as Thine own Self, that found

The ransom for our souls : the love Thou hast

Displayed for fallen man—that doth abound

Even for the deeply fallen!   O that around

Thy throne may soon be gathered millions more

Who grope in heathen darkness, where the sound

Of Christ's blest name none bear, and none adore

Thy glorious majesty, Thy wisdom, love, and power.

99.

"Reclaim the nations, Lord! Bring back the lost—

The wanderers through long ages! From the chain

Of guilt and misery let the captive host

Of heathen men be freed!   O let the reign

Of Thy dear Son begin!   To swell the train

Of His long-promised triumph, let men come,

Who long in degradation dark have lain,

Blinded and maimed, in Superstition's gloom,—

By Christ redeemed,—to share the brightness of our

home!

100.

"It would Thy heart rejoice that they were saved :

It would Thy saints rejoice to see them blest :

O Father, save our race by sin enslaved !

Thy Son hath died Thy holiness to manifest :

Send forth Thy healing Spirit to quell the pest

And plague of sin : Thy saving health dispense

O'er all the earth, till every human breast

Be consecrate to Thee with love intense :

All rebel wills be bowed in sweet obedience !"

101.

Their song was longer ; but a sudden sense

Grew in me that I must not share the sight

O' the City of God, or join the confluence

Into its gates of God's own Martyrs bright,

As heretofore, or scale the mountain's height ;

But must return to earth.

                I woke, to wait

My final call.   Lord, while I strive to fight

The fight of faith, help me to vindicate

Thy truth, and win the fallen from their low estate !

[1] Stanza 39. WINFRED of CREDITON in Devonshire (in the kingdom of Wessex), born in 680 A.D. He was consecrated Bishop, and named BONIFACE by Pope Gregory II., in 723 A.D. His life was written by Willibald, one of his disciples.—See " Life of St. Boniface, Archbishop of Mayence and Apostle of Germany." By the Rev. Geo. W. Cox, S.C.L. London, Joseph Masters : 1853.

[2] Stanza 41. EOBAN and ADALHERE. There were others martyred in Friesland besides Boniface and these two.—For their names, see Cox's " Life of St. Boniface," p. 129.

[3] Stanza 45. JAMES PARNELL. For the cruel martyrdom of this dear young Quaker lad, at Colchester Castle, in 1655—during the Protectorate of Cromwell—see Sewell's " History of the Rise, Increase, and Progress of the Christian People called Quakers."

Stanza 45. EDWARD BURROUGH. Stifled to death in Newgate. For an account of his happy death, and for the eulogium pronounced on him after death, by his friend Howgill, see also Sewell's History.

[5] Stanza 45. RICHARD HUBBERTHORN. Nearly on the same page Sewell relates the death of this devoted servant of Christ, also in Newgate prison.

[6] Stanza 45. JOHN TROWEL. He was so beaten and bruised and crushed, by the Trained Bands of King Charles II., who were sent to break up Quakers' meetings by force, that he died.—See the beginning of the 7th Book of Sewell's History.

[7] Stanza 46. FRANCIS HOWGILL. He died in Appleby gaol, after

five years' imprisonment. His death was peacefully triumphant.—See
the 9th Book of Sewell's History.

[8] Stanza 47. MARY DYAR. Of all the New England Martyrs, this
heroic and holy woman seems to have been the flower. Her death—
after prolonged ill-treatment and suffering—was joyous and exultant.—
See the 5th Book of Sewell's History.

[9] Stanza 48. "Unlyric names." William Robinson, a merchant of
London, and Marmaduke Stevenson of Yorkshire, were condemned to
be hanged along with Mary Dyar. The three went hand in hand,
exultantly, to the gallows. Robinson and Stevenson being dead, Mary
Dyar was ordered to ascend the ladder, which she did readily; but when
they had tied her hands and bandaged her eyes, they told her she was
reprieved. Yet she was executed some months after. The bodies of
Robinson and Stevenson having hung till they were dead, they were cut
down, and thrust *naked* into a hole dug for them at the foot of the
gallows.—See Sewell's 5th Book.

[10] Stanza 48. WILLIAM LEDDRA. He was chained to a log, both
day and night, during a long winter, and in an open prison. He died
with the calmest resignation.—See Sewell's 6th Book.

[11] Stanza 49. "Whipped through New England towns." The barbarous whipping of Elizabeth Hooton, a woman of threescore years of
age, of Anne Colman, of Mary Tomkins, of Alice Ambrose, and
others, is recited also by Sewell in his 6th Book.

BOOK IV.

1.

O FAIR young Moon, if there were nought but thy

Bright crescent to attract men's gaze from earth,

It were enough to make them bless God's sky !

The children love to see thee, and with mirth

Welcome thy coming ; and to Age thy birth,

Anew, is ever gladdening, as a sign

That Nature is not old, but still brings forth

Her undimmed glories, and her gifts benign—

Sustained in during energy by the Hand Divine !

2.

What countless, million-million, mortal eyes

Have watched the swelling of thy silver bow,

Until it grew a shield—then shrank in size,

And vanished, to appear again a show

Of beauty above all stars that sparkling strow
The vault of Night.   With what joy-ravishment
The first young human pair the primal glow
Of thy return first saw!   How oft hath blent
Fears with the hopes of later mortals when was bent,

3.

Once more, thy shining form above their heads,
And corn-fields cried for the reaper, but the rain
Fell, pitiless : the rain that surely sheds
Its torrents by thy fickle leave : the swain
So held it.   And, now men, of science vain,
Disdainfully regard the Past, they hold
It still the same.   Although in thy domain,
They swear, there is no moisture : but a cold,
Dry, lifeless cinder is thy seeming face of gold !

4.

When sweet young eyes so often by thy light—
Blest boon for. lovers ! — wandered to breathe
    sighs

Of tenderness and constancy, a slight

On thy bright form, they would have deemed sur-

    mise

That thou wert aught so mean. With their own

    eyes,

Did they not see that Sabbath-breaking Jew

Who gathered sticks i' the wilderness, his prize

Upon his shoulder, ever exposed to view,

A prisoner in thy orb, rolling amid the blue ?

5.

Argal, in thee there must be living things !—

What, if in thy mild region still dwelt fair,

Though fallen, angels, who with feeble wings

Ventured, sometimes, down through the lower air,

To whisper mortals, and to sin ensnare—

For that they were themselves ensnared, not prime

In sin, and therefore were not doomed to share

Great torment: yet the wish grew, with their

    crime,

To spread for other souls of sin the deadly slime.

6.

But thou the lamp for fairy revels wert,

My grannam said—for her own grannam saw

The little people gaily dance and flirt,

I' the mystic grassy ring, with shivering awe,

And *spake aloud !*—not knowing the mystic law

That would subject her to their mighty power—

To tickle her nose and ears with an oaten straw,

And pinch her sides in sleep ; turn the milk sour

She had left in dirty bowls, and play pranks, hour by

    hour—

7.

All in the night : they had no sunshine game :

 'Twas all by moonshine !   And when they were seen

By mortals *who were silent,* good luck came

To the man or woman.   Gold was found, I ween,

I' their shoon, i' the morning ; if the poor to glean

Went forth in harvest, they would gather sheaves !

The bullfinch would not rob their cherry treen ;

The swallows would build, and twitter, 'neath the

    eaves ;

And luck come naturally as fall the autumn leaves !

8.

Thou wert the patroness of so much good

I' the times of Fancy, that one shrinks to tell,

Fair Moon! how thy account of evil stood;

How thy eclipse foreshadowed griefs to quell

The stoutest heart: shipwreck and storm, and yell

Of drowning sailors; and conspiracy,

Secret and dark, and murderously fell,

'Gainst kings; and overthrow of cities free;

And famine and plague, and every dread calamity!

9.

And was it all a dream, fair shining Moon?

Does thy eclipse forebode nor good nor ill?

Will fairies leave no gold in idlers' shoon?

Are all the fairies gone, and must we till

Our ground with sweat o' the brow, and must we still

Ring out our toil on the anvil, and work on,

Or starve? And, in thy realm, doth no sweet rill

Murmur, or river flow? Is the dream, too, gone,

That angels lived upon thee? Is there never-a-one?

10.

And art thou, seeming splendour of the night,

Only a cinder, lifeless, dark, and cold?

Then we will bless thee for thy borrowed light;

And still more bless the goodness that doth hold

Thee in thy orbit, by the rule untold

Till Newton scanned it, and, thence, safely scanned

The vast mechanic system manifold

Of central wheel and wheels dependent, planned

By God's own wisdom: formed and held by His own

    hand!

11.

"God, acting in His own great universe"—

So, when one asked what Gravitation was,

The immortal sage defined it, in his terse,

Significant way.   He did not care two straws

What critics, foolish and fine, prated of "laws."

He knew that law could not itself maintain:

There must be the Unseen Sustaining Cause,

To ensure the sequence men call "law."   In vain

Even Halley doubt pled often: Newton, with hands

    twain,

12.

Held fast his faith ; and, with a lowly mind

And truthful heart, kept on his wondrous way

To the end.   'Tis not in lowliness mankind

O' the scientific class, in this our day,

Shew greatness.   They their searching wit display

In spying " evolution," everywhere,—

" Selection natural,"—and the sovereign sway

Of what they call " development."   O rare

Development of wit ! what fools our fathers were !

13.

They thought God *could* create, an' if He chose ;

And *had* created.   Sages of science, now,

Shake their small heads, and mutter they suppose

'Twas a mistake !   But, if you ask them how

The universe came to be, they say they trow

'Tis better to say nought : 'tis not for frail,

Imperfect mortals, such as they, to allow

Themselves in airs pretentious the dark veil

From Nature's face to lift—the veil all-mystical !

14.

And this sounds modest ; but men need a rest

Both for the heart and mind.   No Godless creed—

If one may call it so—can ease the breast

In trouble ; or the heart's affections feed

With satisfaction ; or within us breed

Resolve to battle with temptation strong

To moral evil.   Surely, no great greed

A man will feel to conquer sin, so long

As he believes not in the Judge of right and wrong.

15.

I would not hastily condemn.   God knows

I have great cause, remembering errors past,

To shun hot speech. But why this prate of " laws,"

And "reverence " for them ?   Each encomiast

Of our grandees of science utters fast

And loud his praises for their championship

Of Truth.   But what is their Truth worth ?   A vast

Dim waste of words it seems to me to skip

From sequence unto sequence, and yet never grip

16.

The deeper Truth—that there must be a Cause
For all this sequence, though it ever be
As *fixed* as they assert it is.   No "laws"
Are known by stones or trees, by sky or sea ;
Nor can they, senseless, pay a penalty
For disobedience.   Men discern full well
They break a law when pain or misery
Succeeds an act.   Rocks, trees, or waters tell
No sinners' tale of suffering, for they ne'er rebel.

17.

God makes a law for free-willed essences—
Angels or men.   Man in the plenitude
Of regal power ; or, where true freedom is,
Men representative make laws, and rude
Rebellion 'gainst them brings on humble and proud—
Or should bring—penalty most sure.   We all
Admire right law, and sensibly conclude
Them wise that made such law ; but never call
A law its own enactor.   Why should mortals fall

18.

In " reverence " before sequence which they deem
The " law of Nature " ?   Surely we should rise
Above such heathenism, and God supreme
Over His realm of Nature recognize,
Nor dare to say His power to the All-wise,
Almighty One is *fixed*.

               The summer air
Invites.   I have performed my exercise
Of Duty, and should sleep ; but they so fair
And bright appear—the beauteous stars!—that I must
    share

19.

The glorious sight, once more.   How full of life
Must be the world-stored universe of God !
Yon glittering splendours cannot be unrife
With conscious being.   Each sphere is surely trod
By moral agents : not the mean abode
Of animal natures only.   'Twere to deem
God's work unworthy of Himself to load
Immensity with suns, if every beam
They shed, however bright, shewed only Death supreme ;

20.

Or, merely forms that simply live and feel,

But neither know, nor thought reflective share.

Creatures, God made to inherit bounteous weal,

According to their natures ; and His care

Of all shews that His wisdom deems them fair ;

Yet, higher joy must fill God's holy mind

Looking on Man, than on the forms most rare

In outward beauty to the earth assigned,

That are to all earth's truly beautiful so blind.

21.

And, if the all-bounteous Father doth feel joy

In giving life, and higher joy the more

He gives of higher life, nought should destroy

Our love of life.   To deem the gift but poor—

The highest gift that God, the Great Bestower,

Can give, is surely base ; and baser still

It is to wish Death should our being devour.

Thank God ! I never felt such wish : no ill

With hatred of existence could my bosom fill.

22.

I love existence.   And I would not die,

Although I'm old, except to live again,

And think, and feel, and know, and satisfy

My being with comprehending what all men

On earth can only apprehend.   The ken

All-spiritual I long to have—the gaze

Angelic, gleaning, at once, what in this den

Of clay-bound mind we cannot reach, though days

And years be spent in trying to pierce the Stygian haze.

23.

And yet, how know we that the essences

Of things are better known to angels than

To men?   Man knows most surely that he is ;

But knows not what he is.   Can angels scan

Their own existence, through and through, with span

And compass of familiarity,

And say, "We know ourselves"? No more than man,

I trow, can aught created boast, with glee,

" We've found it !   Come and shout with us !   We've
    found the key

24.

"That unlocks Mystery ! What Life is we know ;
And knowing what Life is, shall we not make
Things that shall live ? " Yet *they* most hotly glow
With fervency of trust that *they* shall take
God's work out of His mighty hands, and wake
Up matter dead to life, some morning bright,
Ere long.   It was of our sage men I spake—
Darwin, and Huxley, and Tyndal—each a light
Of lustrous mind who sheds from such empyreal height

25.

On lowly men that still grope in the dark,
And say they cannot through a millstone look,
Except by the hole i' the midst. "But, when the spark
Electric hath the protoplasma strook,
The secret will not our sage Huxley hook,
And wake dead matter up, as he designed ? "—
Think ye, the knife when Simple Simon took
To cut his mother's bellows open, and find
What made them blow, the philosophe *did* find the
    wind ?

26.

"As gods ye shall be !" said the snake to Eve ;
And still man whispers it to his own ear.
And, while he doubts so much he should believe
With childlike simpleness, he feels no fear
To grasp his Maker's attributes, or near
Approach to make, at least, to what God's hand
Alone can do.   I would not tarry here
To learn such "science," though they call it "grand ;"
But, for right aims, I still would live in Fatherland.

27.

Not many have seen more of it than I :
Its hills and vales and woods ; its streams, its strand ;
Its quaint old cities, and its hamlets shy ;
Its crowded, gay, new towns bizarrely planned ;
Its moated castles, and its abbeys grand
In ruin, with its proud cathedralled piles.
Through shire and hundred, over Fatherland,
On foot, by wain, on steed, what merry miles
I've sped !   The thought with pleasure still my heart
    beguiles.

28.

I love existence. Never can return

The hours of youth or manhood ; but I feel

'Tis pleasant, oft, to let the mind disurn

The Dead beloved, and bring them back to seal

Old friendships o'er again ; to think o' the zeal

We felt in our debates—the merriment—

The fire—the fun—the wish the hour to steal

Past midnight : then, the grave rebuke swift sent

From brows of senior, "take-care!" men—so eloquent!

29.

I thank the Almighty Maker that I've lived,

And feel life hath been blessèd. What, though
    pain

Hath mingled with my ease ? I have not grieved

At pain so much as at my inward stain

Of sin and guilt. My life hath been, i' the main,

A pleasant pilgrimage. I cannot hold

With him who scorns this life, as but a vain

And worthless dream, soon over and soon told :

A dream that doth mere changes of a dream unfold.

30.

Life hath been real to me ; real in its joy,

And in its sorrow.   And the reality

Of life I would not lose.   No pleasures cloy

In life that men name rightly.   If their free

Heritage of choice men will abuse, yet see

The issue must be punishment, the blame

Is justly theirs.   Men know the high decree

That links their sin with punishment and shame,

And know their arguments against it halt and lame.

31.

The men I knew who said, " There is no sin :

Creatures of circumstance men are ; and praise

And blame are follies"—I ever heard begin

To praise and blame, if to forget their craze

You could beguile them.   In the startling days

Of forty-eight, old Robert Owen said

His solemn say, very oft—"He but betrays

His folly who blames and praises."   Ere his head

Was turned, he praised and blamed the living and the

dead !

32.

I well remember how his new-found friend,

Young Louis Blanc—an exile—sat by his side,

At Ashburner's, the opening and the end

Comparing, of his speech.   Puzzled, he tried

To unravel it, but failed.   I had to hide

My face for laughter.   But, the old man's look

Was quite triumphant ; and he glanced with pride

Around,—as who should say, " No sovereign duke,

Or king, can match my greatness : I no equal brook !"

33.

Self-worship was his foible—nay, his sin !

And all his followers to the top of his bent

Befooled and flattered him ; and did but grin

At others for born fools who shewed they lent

No ear to Robert's teaching.   No dissent

Was borne with.   *His* was the name o' the Age !

" The Age of Owen" 'twould be called when blent

With dust he was !   They told him so !   The sage

Nodded,—as he would say, " That's true, a crown I'll

wage !"

34

So proud at heart—and yet how meek and kind

He was, even when the storm of anger swelled

Around him !   Imperturbable his mind

In contest seemed, when younger ; but he held

His head up loftily, in age, and quelled

Dissent with words that showed he deemed men low

In intellect who could not see he excelled

All teachers of his time.   So surely grow

Proud thoughts in man whose fellows weakly to him

    bow !

35.

Yet, one feels glad to have known a man that drew

Thousands around him who became so sure

That what he taught was truth.   Alas ! how few

Are able to resist a panic !   Be the lure

Substance or shadow, when the calenture

Sets in, the human sheep begin to run ;

And, soon, all run who see the race !   Impure,

Unholy license seemed a precious boon

To fools.   Some saw their folly ere life's task was

    done ;

36.

But Owen never changed, or faltered. From

The outset of his course he seemed possessed

Of rocklike strength of will. The masterdom

Of all men's ills should yield to his behest,

He told the crowds. They could suspect no jest :

He gave his wealth, his time, to spread the scheme

Of Socialism. He never seemed distrest

At failure ; and when others ceased to dream

Of winning Eden back to earth, and said no gleam

37.

They saw o' the promised light, he widely stared,

And said he wondered, for the light was full—

Nay, fuller than the sun's own light it glared :

The triumph was at hand : their eyes were dull

Who could not see the signs of it. No lull

Of earnestness he showed for fourscore years ;

And, in old age, he said nought could annul

His triumph : it was come ! They gave him cheers :

He was stone-deaf : I do not think they reached his

ears.

38.

Owen has gone ; and, with him, too, his sect.

And Communism hath, once more, had its day

Of murderous rule, in Paris !   All bedeckt

With beauty was their city, when a stay

But brief I made in it—although the fray

O' the Reds with Cavaignac was barely o'er,

And their new President did not display

His purpose to be Emperor yet.   She wore

Her splendour still—the famous city—as of yore.

39.

Frenchmen were proud of Paris—even the poor,

As were the rich : they hurled no monument down,

Although they soaked the stones with human gore.

The column in the Place Vendôme no frown

Provoked—the Louvre's array of art no groan

Evoked of hatred from the workmen-bands

That struck for broader freedom.   Now the tone

Of Labour's sons is changed.   They say the sands

I' the glass of Privilege are spent: all with their hands

40

Or heads shall labour, for the future. " Pride

And idleness should have no rest," they said ;

And so they burned their city, and defied

All retribution ! Though their land had bled

Beneath the Prussian's proud revengeful tread,

They turned to shed each other's blood ! The old

Mad zest for civil strife is still misbred

Within them. God forbid we should their mould

So fratricidal take—'midst changes manifold !

For change hath come in England that I deemed

Unlikely yet to come, for many a year ;

And other changes threaten. It had seemed

Great cause, indeed, for joy to me to hear

Some changes had been wrought ; but now a fear

Checks my new joy that License soon may come—

Wild License, rather than the triumph dear

Of Liberty, in this dear isle, her home

So long—where all her exiled sons find welcome room !

42.

After such midnight musings, slumber came.
And, soon, the wakeful mind—as a player would say—
Caught up her cue from these last thoughts, to frame
Her converse in my sleep.

            I dreamt my way
I took again, in Paradise, where lay
Familiar flowers : the bell-flower tall and fair,
That blooms by rocky Tees, even near the spray
Of the High Force : grass of Parnassus rare
In beauty—nay, most beautiful beyond compare!—

43.

That decks the banks of forkèd Tyne,
Where he turns south, by old quaint Alston, high
Above all towns in perch,—and where, with fine
Sense of the beautiful—(sure, bending nigh,
The angels whisper them !)—one child doth vie
With another in reverence for the fresh " God-flower"—
For so they name it !   And that living eye,
Or star of the earth—the Trientalis—dower
Of loveliness—that one would gaze at, hour by hour!

44.

It grows in the park of Alnwick—but we found
It first in Scotland—I and my Love—near chill
But cheerful Grantown, where frail flowers abound :
The fairy orchis, with its infantile
And chaste white florets : pyrolas that thrill
The soul with wonder at their gracefulness ;
While gymnadenias rich perfume distil
Around your heathery path ; and lady's tress
Renders your power to name its beauty languageless

45.

I dreamt such flowers I found, but each enhanced
In delicate grace of form, richness of scent,
And bloom, till, as before, I seemed entranced
To ecstasy, amid such lavishment
Of loveliness and sweetness. ' But soon lent
I hearing to the voice I dreamt I heard
Of one discoursing in a strain that sent
Strange vigour through me, as when one doth gird
Himself for fight—for fiery words his blood have
    stirred.

46.

I knew it was the voice of Claude Brousson,[1]

" The Evangelist of the Desert "—martyr brave,

Who, strangled on the wheel, with soul so strong

Met death, at Montpellier, when Louis drave

From France its holiest sons—himself the slave

Of Rome, although " Magnificent " proclaimed—

Louis "le grand Monarque "—to whose blood clave

The vengeance of the Lord, when men's hearts flamed .

With hate of kings, and Pride and Privilege were tamed.

47.

With Claude walked other martyrs by the wheel :

Dumas, and Fulcran Rey, Guion, Bonnemere,

And Olivier Souverain,[2]—who all with leal

Fidelity and readiness did bear

Their torture, and escaped to Christ.   Their share

Of bliss these now were reaping ; and with them

A crowd beside of brothers, each now heir

Of Jesu's heaven.   And all seemed, in my dream,

Intently listening to the Desert Preacher's theme.

48.

"Brothers," spake Claude, "regird the loins o' the mind;
And still take heart that we the combat keep
With Rome's dark falsehood—though we find
Her power so strong, her hold so wide and deep
O'er human hearts, when we descend the steep
To earth, on God's great errands.   Let us hold
His promise fast—that He will call His sheep,
In every land, into Truth's holy fold :
Let us hold firmly by His word proclaimed of old ! "

49.

He paused, as if reluctant to speak on,
From large emotion,—while his brethren held
His form in silent deep observance.   Soon,
The fact to me was mystically revealed
That Claude, but now, had from his ancient field
Of warfare and of suffering journeyed home,
Again, to heaven ; and had not yet unsealed
His later knowledge, whether the day of doom
They waited for so long had come for slaughterous Rome.

50.

"Tell us, loved brother, if our own loved France"—
With meek impetuousness, spake Fulcran Rey—
"Have left the spectacle—the song—the dance—
Her boast of victories—and begun to pray.
We learned that there the priest had lost his sway
O'er men, though women seek his benison.
We wait to know that Frenchmen change their gay
And volant life, for earnestness. Soon gone
Will be Rome's power, if Frenchmen grave and pious
    have grown."

51.

"Ye marked my hesitance," Brousson replied ;
"I cannot tell ye that our France grows wise,
Or pious. Still she keeps her boastful pride
And vanity—although the Prussian dyes
Her soil with blood, and still for vengeance cries,
Remembering the dread wrong he suffered while
The wasteful Corsican won victories
Like sports, and fed his eager hosts on spoil,
And humbled kings, as if they were but peasants vile.

52.

" I deem, my brother, that thou judgest right :

Rome's day is gone when France casts off her yoke

In earnest, and no longer, in loose plight

Affects to wear it, as a masterstroke

Of policy.   When neither jest, nor joke,

France makes of Christian truth, but with the force

Of all the reason that she boasts, the Book

Reads for herself, and reads with the remorse

Of conscience, she will soon break down the Papal

   curse.

53.

" But, even now, Rome seeks on her to lean :

Fallen Rome on conquered France ! The old man

   shorn

Of territory and civil rule, with keen

And smarting sense of the Italians' scorn—

For oft they jest around his nest forlorn,—

His petty realm—the City Leonine,

Across the Tiber—still uplifts his horn

Of pride, and dares to mutter curse malign

On all his foes ; and frets till France doth give the sign

54.

" That she will yet befriend him—for no friend
He hath 'mong reigning potentates : none heed
His blessing or his curse.   Some think their end—
The end of kings—is near, and feel they need
To care most for themselves, since treasons breed
So fast around them ; while the stronger strive
To strengthen more their thrones—ignoring creed
And faith—by following plans preventative,
They think, of revolution : for they now perceive

55.

"The earthquake threatens, throughout Europe broad,
From Labour's children, who so small a share
Of good gain for themselves, although they load
Others with plenty, by their skill, and toil, and care.
The earthquake threatens ; and so, hosts for war
The strong kings train by myriads, armed with new
And deadlier weapons ; and auxiliar
Artillery, more deadly still, now through
The air whirls weights of metal such as men ne'er
knew,

56.

" Or heard of, since the warring world began ;

And ships are clad with iron plates, immense

In thickness,—and impelled with hurricane

Velocity, by force of steam, intense.

Thus, horrible destruction, at expense

Enormous, emperor, and king, and czar

Make ready, confident, when Turbulence

Sounds trumpet, with the giant game of war

To wield off revolution, or subdue its jar !

57.

" Our own loved France—now bruised and bleeding

     France—

Raves, too, of warlike preparation, quick,

Like conquering kings—nay, with an arrogance

The nations round deem nought but lunatic,

Boasts her revenge shall come, and she will strike

Her foes with such paralysis of fear,

They at her feet shall crawl, and, trembling, lick

The dust !   To pray, didst ask, my brother dear,

If France had now begun ?   Such tidings we shall hear

58.

"From earth, in God's own time, I trust.   But prayer

Is farthest from her thought—of all the thought·

That enters human minds, when filled with care,

And torn with sorrow, for the suffering brought

To their own doors, upon their hearths, about

Their beds—sorrow o'erwhelming to the mass

Of men—but sorrow Frenchmen learn to flout

With merriment, and mockery, and grimace !

Oh, when, great God, shall reason truly mark our race!"

59.

Silent, the Martyrs walked, when Brousson ceased,

In holy sorrow, till Bonnemere thus spake :

"And who hath ruined France ? who, but the

     priest—

What, but the subtle power of the fell Snake

Of Rome—did first the strength of Frenchmen break

Under the yoke ?   How long and bravely strove

Our grand forerunners, who the chain, and stake,

And fiery flame, with spirit of the dove

Endured—blessing their foes who them with fury drove

60.

"From life, although their lives to France had been
Unmeasured good! How long we strove—our aim
How pure—God truly knows! The haughty, unclean,
Yet worshipt king—the pride, and yet the shame,
Of France!—yielded, at last, to play Rome's game
To the full; and, in expelling from his land
Its Christian people, struck the blow to maim
Its industry and wealth: his court, so grand,
Robbed Poverty of its bread with unrelenting hand;

61.

"And vice and waste became the heritage
Of his doomed house, till Misery rose with fell
And fierce revenge to crush out Privilege!
And still they hear the voice of vengeance swell
Above the roar of war; and who shall spell
When it shall cease?"—
              "And when from France the true
Disciples of the Lord were driven"—to tell
His thought, Dumas began—"the Atheist crew
Soon gave the tone to court, and crowd, and science, too.

62.

"When nought was left to represent the faith

Of Christ, but mass idolatrous—the bread

Turned into Deity by the noisome breath,

Perchance, of some foul priest, and overhead

Held up for worship ; while the incense spread

Its odour round ; and eunuch songsters strained

Their hireling throats, by opera music led ;

And cloth of gold unto the priest pertained,

While rags scarce clad the peasant whom the Church

    had drained

63.

"Of his last mite—what wonder that the minds

Of men revolted with disgust from show

And showman too ?   Few, now, the forgery blinds,

'Mong Frenchmen ; but men much more easily throw

Their idols down than learn to humbly bow

'Fore sovran Truth.   Oh that the Lord would raise

Up for Himself, in France, some teacher low

In men's esteem, but who with Truth's pure blaze

Should fire French souls, till they proclaim the

    Saviour's praise !"

64.

"God hath His witnesses, though few "—in haste,

Spake Claude : " a remnant of our race give ear

And heart unto the truth.   They have embraced

Its teachings from the stranger, and hold dear

The word of life.   Brethren, we will not fear !

Their number shall increase, till France shall be

Among the foremost nations that revere

The Crucified ; and, over land and sea,

Her sons shall champion the new Christian Chivalry !"

65.

"Lord, let Thy servant's faith be realized

Right early ! "—prayed the Martyr company,

Aloud;—and sounds that shewed some sympathised

With them, in Paradise, were heard.   The three

Brothers Du Plans[3] approached, with holy glee

"Amen " responding : with them, David Quet,[4]

And elder martyrs twain—Pierre de Bruis,[5]

And Henri, "the false hermit,"[6] as the men of prey

Misnamed their victim, in the famed St. Bernard's day.

13

66.

And, after these, drew near a Martyr crowd—
A crowd innumerous—that on earth were named
With many names—some given by wicked, proud,
And persecuting men ; and some that epigrammed
Their virtues.   They who, when the faggots flamed
Around their limbs, at Lyons, aloud exclaimed
They saw the heavens opened ; and, at Toulouse,
Where met, i' the Middle Age, the Council famed
For persecution, they whom its foul abuse
Meekly received, and dared its sentence murderous.

67.

And they who bled or burnt, for stubborn faith,
In Gascogne, and Provence, and Dauphiné ;
And, in Lorraine and Picardy, met death
Exultantly: some called " The Men that pray,"
And some "The Men that sing:" some termed the stray
Dwellers with wolves, or Turlupins.   The poor
That loved them called them "pure"—Cathari: they—
The proud—who hated them, never forbore
To give them names of guilt, without a metaphor.

68.

Poor Men, Poor Weavers, Publicans,
Beghards, Beguines, and Manichees, some chose
To call them, as they wandered o'er the plains
Of sunny France, or climbed the Alpine snows,
Or hid in Pyrenæan vales from foes ;
And Albigenses were they called, who fell
In thousands by De Montfort's sword[7]—the blows
Approved by Rome, who said the work was well
And nobly done : work worthy of the fiends of hell !

69.

Anon, joined these, another Martyr host :
The Vaudois of Provence, whom fierce Oppéde[8]
'Slew with the sword, or burnt—a holocaust
To glut his bad revenge—the slaughter made
By order of the king, won by the aid
Of Cardinal de Tournon : penitent
In death, the royal Francis strongly bade
Henri, his son, to follow with punishment
The guilty deed : a charge to which dull heed was lent.

70.

The gathered Martyr companies of France

That lived, on earth, some centuries apart,

Yet gave each other the fraternal glance,

And seemed a mighty army of one heart.

Forthwith, in serried ranks they formed athwart

The flowery plain, as if their wont to meet

Thither, it were—not to record the smart

Of their past martyrdom, but one to greet

Another, and rehearse old earthly memories sweet.

71.

Their greetings all renewed, the waving Hand

Of Light again appeared above.   All saw

The signal, and the universal band

Struck up the song of praise and love and awe,

With mingled prayer for France—the holy law

Obeying which, in Paradise, doth bind

All souls from earth, and did them thither draw,

To pray their Lord for those still left behind,

In Fatherland, that they may all His mercy find.

72.

"Great God of might, who dost all worlds possess—

Creator of our being—Redeemer strong

From sin—and Sanctifier who dost men bless

With heart-renewal, and grace to leave the wrong

And cleave unto the right!   Again, our song

We raise—our brother-song of grateful joy—

That, though we grieved Thy holiness so long,

In mortal life, Thou didst not us destroy ;

But didst preserve our souls to share Thy blest

  employ!

73.

" O Holy Lord, make bare Thy sovran arm,

And from our Fatherland old Error chase!

No longer let the priest, with baneful charm,

Delude men's souls ! No longer let our race

Give up their souls to folly and foul embrace

Of deadliest sin !   Thy power to humble pride,

O Lord, Thou hast displayed before their face,

With awful force, and still Thou dost them chide—

But, by their blinded eyes Thy hand is undescried.

74.

"O God, let men, throughout the humbled realm

Of France, begin to think—until from off

Their eyes the scales shall fall, and shame o'er-
>   whelm

Their souls that they so long have lived to scoff

At things Divine, and to deride all proof

Of Thine Existence, who so long hast borne

With their foul sin.   Let Frenchmen keep aloof

No longer from Thy Christ!   Oh, let their scorn

Of meekness end!   Lord, beam upon their souls
>   forlorn!"

75.

The prayerful song went on—the fervid plea

For France, that God would cleanse her mental sight

From folly's films, her veil of vanity

Remove, restore her spirit from the blight

Of scepticism, and fill it with the bright

Perception that in Christ is true repose—

Repose her restless spirit needs to upknit

Her ravelled strength,—to still her strifeful throes,—

And a transcendent future for her sons disclose.

76.

Their prayer harmonious ended ; when began

The brethren towards the terraced hills to wend,

In serried ranks.   The Martyr caravan,

Triumphant marching, did its wings extend

Across the plain till the low hills ascend

I, erst, saw in my dream : the river's marge

It also touched ; and often seemed to bend

Its lines by the winding river : space so large

It filled.—But, now, I heard one Mind new thoughts

    discharge.

77.

'Twas one whose flesh by pincers was torn off—

Bold John le Clerc,[9] they martyred in Lorraine,

For that, with fiery zeal, beneath the roof

Papists called holy he broke their idols vain

To pieces.   To the few I saw remain—

Brousson, Bonnemere, and Dombres [10]—I heard him say

" My brothers, we can never here complain

Of what doth seem the All-wise One's delay

In saving France ; but, how mysterious seems His way !

78.

" He leaves the land which so much martyrs' blood
Hath consecrated, and where Mind hath won
Its proudest triumphs,—in its hardihood
Of unbelief and pride to wander on ;—
And seeks the barbarous races 'neath the sun :
The dwellers on the islands of the sea,
And far-off continents, but dimly known
When we were sharers of mortality—
Lo ! while I speak, the new-born spirits hither flee !—

79.

" For Sin with Holiness the war on earth
Will wage till comes the end, and ever slake
Its thirst with blood of Saints—yea, count it mirth
To see their bodies writhe with torturous ache,
Or burning.   So, some hither from the stake
Now come, and some slain by the piercing spear ;
And from the rock let fall to earth, where brake
Their bones, others have come.   Welcome, ye dear
Disciples of our Lord !—We give ye heavenly cheer !"

80.

" Welcome, dear brethen, from the island far,

To Jesu's Paradise !" aloud Brousson

And his companions cried ; "ye welcome are

To all God's Saints !"

                I knew this Martyr throng

From Madagascar came—the island, long

And broad, the channel named the Mozambique

Divides from Afric land.   Victims of wrong

They felt they were, and did no pardon seek,

But met their death with joy, and Christian courage

   meek.

81.

Victims of Ranavalona[11]—savage queen—

A demon-legion seemed to fill and rule,

As when Christ dwelt on earth, the spirits unclean

Possessed the man : the evil spirits so foul,

That, driven out of man, they begged control

O'er filthy swine, and gained their strange request—

Christ—as the Judge of men—letting the shoal

Of swine be drowned, His mind to manifest—

The Jews, by keeping them, Jehovah's law trangressed.

82.

Sisters there were, as well as brethren, in

The island Martyr band.   The queen so vile

Spared neither her own sex, nor her own kin.

The maiden Rasalama,[12] with a smile—

As proto-martyr of her native isle—

Led on the Christian company.   Her hand

She gave to Rafaralahy,[13] the youth who while

They led her forth to death, with bravery grand

Walked with her as she sang—spite of the queen's
    command.

83.

Full soon it was his turn to die.   They slew

Him as he knelt where her unburied bones

Were strewed.   And more they killed.   I fear, all new

Ye would their names proclaim, and strange the tones,

If I pronounced them!   Few to their death groans

Gave heed, in England—where the boast

Is rife—"There are no Martyrs now." "The moans"—

Say ye?—"were faint on that far southern coast"?

Truly, full oft their moans in hymns of joy were lost!

84.

" Sing us, sweet sister," spake Brousson, "the hymn

We heard that thou didst sing when thou wert led

To martyrdom."[14]   To me her words were dim :

The melody with windings seemed to thread

The spiritual air, till—as the great one said—

With " linkèd sweetness long drawn out," the mind

O'erpowered seemed tears of tenderness to shed,

With rapturous thrill.   Thus sounds are intertwined

With feeling, whether in earth or heaven, for human-

   kind !

85.

Then sang the Malagasy, in their tongue,

And with like tenderness, in joyous strains,

And in full chorus, other hymns they sung

In their late days of martyrdom and pain.

Their music rose above the flowery plain,

Until I saw the infant company

Of Welcomers gather in troops, amain,

And float o'erhead, and list with ecstasy

And wonder, what the music, new to heaven, might be.

86.

And then, in spiritual tongue, the men of France
Spake with the Malagasy of the time
Of persecution—when no sustenance
They gat, for days, i' the woods, and had to climb
Rude rocks, and hide in caves, or in the slime
Of swamps, to escape their hunters; and the hate
O' the wicked queen to flee : their only crime
They worshipped Christ, and would not fall prostrate
'Fore blocks of wood by ignorant heathen consecrate.

87.

With grateful joy the Malagasy told
How first the missionary-men to preach
Began, and how some felt that truth gat hold
Of all their heart ; and when by signs to teach—
By printed signs as well as spoken speech—
The men began, what wonder, and what zeal
Some felt to learn until their minds could reach
The meaning of God's word, and sweetly feel
What great salvation for their souls it did reveal.

88.

And how they hid its precious leaves, when raged

Fierce Ranavalona, and nightly drew them forth

From their concealment, and by stealth assuaged

Their thirst for the living water: how i' the earth

They hid Christ's printed truth, and with what mirth

They dug it up when none of all their foes

Were nigh.   And then, how great they deemed the
worth

Of Bunyan's Pilgrim-story¹⁵ to disclose

Their hearts began—yea, told of it with rapt applause !

89.

"O brethren, these are wondrous ways of God !"

Said Claude ; "how know we but this savage isle—

For such was Madagascar, when we trod

The soil of earth—may, in the Future, smile

Triumphantly o'er Hellas, and the land of Nile—

Yea, over Europe's proudest boast of art

And science ?   Oft doth God select the vile,

In men's esteem, to enact a lofty part :—

What, if this isle be set down in some future chart

90.

"O' the world, as the pre-eminent Christian seat

Of knowledge and refinement?   God may bring

Judgment upon the nations that maltreat

His truth, and deem it false ; that madly wring

From intellect and sensual revelling,

Alike, the dregs of pleasure ; and ignore

Their Maker's name ; yea, proudly backward fling

His benefits, and call them curses.   O'er

Our ancient home awful judicial change may lour ! "

91.

"Cast not away blest hope !" with cheery shout,

Cried one who led another band in view,

While thus the Preacher spoke of fear and doubt,

And to the terraced mountains nearer drew

The Malagasy and the friendly few

That journeyed with Brousson.   The Martyr band

That now approached, thus cheerily led, I knew,

By mystic insight, were of Gallic land,

Likewise : its ancient Martyrs : they who bore the

brand

92.

Of infamy, when pagan Rome held rule,

And savagely shed Christian blood for game,

By scourge and torture so unpitiful,

'Twere hard to tell: worse than the fiery flame!

And dread exposure, 'mid the loud acclaim

Of thousands, to the claws and teeth of beasts

Wild from their scorching Afric clime : no shame

They felt to boast refinement, yet such feasts

They held i' th' amphitheatres, with brutal jests

93.

Mocking frail woman's sufferings, as of men

The groans. 'Twas Polycarp's disciple[16] led

Gaul's ancient martyrs. He who in Vienne

Was slain. And, with him, they whose blood was
    shed

So recklessly in Lyons, by the dread

Decree of Antoninus Verus, blythely trod

The floral way : Pothinus, whom from bed

They dragged—the man of ninety—to give God

His dying testimony, and seal it with his blood ; [17]

94.

Sanctus, the deacon, stout, defiant, brave,

Amidst all threats and tortures; Attalus,

Maturus, Vettius, and the female slave,

Blandina [18]—noblest martyr for the cross

Of all her sex, in times iniquitous;

And many more.

    " Cast not away blest hope! "

Cried Irenæus; "still remain for us

God's patience and His love.   Let us look up,

My brethren, yet, for fallen France!   Let not faith droop

95.

" While the great Intercessor pleads in heaven,

And saints on earth.   Asunder, God the veil

Of scepticism will rive, as He hath riven

The veil of heathenism!   France shall the trail

O' the serpent see, ere long, and humbly wail

In penitence, that she so long hath held

The false for true, for pure the bestial:

Shall mourn she hath the power of Evil swelled;

And grieve 'gainst God and Christ she hath so long

  rebelled !

96.

" Cast not away blest hope ! " again he cried.

" Blest hope we may not, will not cast away ! "

Cried all the Martyr company ; " Christ died

For sceptic, as for heathen, Gaul : her day

Of grace is not yet past : full soon the ray

Of holiest Truth, with soul-awakening might,

May beam upon her.   Send it, Lord, we pray !

Let France no longer be a realm of night ;

But shine among the nations, by Thy Gospel light ! "

97.

The prayer and song went on, as now to climb

The terraced mountains they began ; the song

Went on—and other songs, with chaunt sublime,

The joyous myriads sang—the happy throng

That, marching, climbed the height with step so

  - strong

And limber : age and weakness felt no more !

They climbed—but sense that I might not prolong

My visit to that realm grew, as before,

Within me ; and I woke to find myself on shore

98.

Of earth, a pilgrim still : Death's mystic sea

Uncrossed !   Yet, I must cross it soon : the years

Must now be scanty that remain for me

On th' hither side o' the tomb.   Life onward wears

Happily, thank God !   Scarcely a "vale of tears "

This life hath been for me.   Still let me prove

My happiness in DUTY : then, no fears

Cold Death can bring : 'twill be but a remove

From happy life below, to happier life above !

NOTES TO BOOK IV.

[1] Stanza 46. CLAUDE BROUSSON, "the Evangelist of the Desert."—See a good, compact life of him, published by Hamilton, Adams and Co. 1853. The Preface is signed by "Henry S. Baynes."

[2] Stanza 47. DUMAS, FULCRAN REY, GUION, BONNEMERE, OLIVIER SOVERAIN, and other martyrs of Montpellier.—Their deaths are all described in the volume I have just mentioned.

[3] Stanza 65. The three brothers, DU PLANS: co-workers also with Claude Brousson.

[4] Stanza 65. DAVID QUET. Broken on the wheel at Montpellier.—For a record of his martyrdom see also the "Life of Claude Brousson."

[5] and [6] Stanza 65. PIERRE DE BRUIS and HENRI, "the FALSE HERMIT."—See some account of their labours and martyrdom in a translation of Antoine Monastier's "History of the Vaudois Church," published by the Religious Tract Society.

[7] Stanza 68. SIMON DE MONTFORT.—One hundred thousand crusaders (and some say more) in 1209, ravaged Languedoc, and slaughtered countless "heretics," under the leadership of Simon de Montfort, and Amalric, the Abbot of Citeaux, and legate of Pope Innocent III.

[8] Stanza 69. The BARON OPPEDE. The merciless butcheries, devastations, and nameless horrors executed upon the poor Vaudois of Provence, under the fierce leadership of this man, are vigorously related in a crowded volume entitled "History of the Protestants of France," etc., by G. de Felice. Translated by P. E. Barnes. Routledge and Co. 1853.

Stanza 77. "Bold JOHN LE CLERC," the woolcomber of Meaux, is an observable figure among the martyrs of France. "In his zeal against the deceiving errors which he saw abounding on every hand, he involved himself and the good cause he had at heart in common ruin, by rashly offending the most cherished prejudices of the prevailing creed. The inhabitants of Metz, whither he had withdrawn, were accustomed annually to repair in crowds on an appointed festival to a neighbouring chapel, where a statue of the Virgin, with others of favourite saints, were the objects of special devotion to the credulous and ignorant populace.

"Like Paul of old, the spirit of Le Clerc was stirred within him to see the city thus wholly given to idolatry; and, forgetful of the example of the apostle in like circumstances, he repaired at an early hour to the church, and breaking the images in pieces, he scattered them before the altar. Though no one witnessed the daring sacrilege, Le Clerc had no desire to flee. The act was designed as a testimony against the sin in which the people were preparing to unite; and when he was dragged before the judges by an enraged multitude, who could hardly be restrained from tearing him in pieces, he fearlessly proclaimed to them Jesus Christ as the sole object of rightful worship.

"The courageous confessor was sentenced to be burned alive; but even a death so horrible could not satisfy his enraged executioners. He was mutilated and torn with red-hot pincers, and his sufferings were prolonged with the most savage ingenuity; after which the sentence of his judges was carried into execution by burning him in a slow fire. . . . While his executioners tore his flesh, and mutilated his face, in a manner too horrible for description, he solemnly ejaculated the words—'*Their idols are silver and gold, the work of men's hands. They that make them are like unto them: so is every one that trusteth in them. O Israel, trust thou in the Lord: He is thy help and thy shield.*'"

¹⁰ Stanza 77. DOMBRES. He and Boisson, both colleagues of Claude de Brousson, went to martyrdom, at Nismes, singing the praises of God, and "finished their course with joy."

¹¹ Stanza 81. RANAVALONA, Queen of Madagascar.—How this woman, who had no rightful claim to the throne, seized it, on the death of King Radama, has been related in English periodicals many times. The reader will find a compact account of the Malagasy martyrs in the

"Narrative of the Persecution of the Christians in Madagascar," etc., by the Missionaries Freeman and Johns. London : Snow, 35, Paternoster Row ; as also in "Madagascar : its Mission and its Martyrs," published by the same house.

[12] Stanza 82. RASALAMA.—The calm, but glorious death of this protomartyr of Madagascar is beautifully told in the last-mentioned little volume.

[13] Stanza 82. RAFARALAHY. "My sister, I will not leave you to the end," said this young man, separating himself from the crowd to walk by the side of Rasalama, as she was led to death. A few days afterwards he, also, was martyred.

[14] Stanza 84. The Malagasy martyrs all went, singing hymns of praise, to the place of death. This so enraged their persecutors, that at last they stuffed straw into the mouths of the sufferers.

[15] Stanza 88. "Bunyan's Pilgrim story."—It was translated into Malagasy by Mr. Johns, the Missionary ; and soon the natives prized it next the Bible.

[16] Stanza 93. "Polycarp's disciple"—IRENÆUS. He was martyred at Vienne, in Gaul, A.D. 202, in the persecution under Severus.

[17] Stanza 93. POTHINUS.—See *Eusebius*, Book v. c. 1.

[18] Stanza 94. SANCTUS the deacon, ATTALUS, MATURUS, VETTIUS EPAGATHUS, BLANDINA, and others.—See *Eusebius*, Book v. c. 1.

BOOK V.

I.

THE winter's sun beams bright, as if 'twere spring,

Gladdening the waters of the lonely sea :

Lonely as death : not even a bird on wing :

No glimpse of man, or boat : a jubilee

Of silence and of death, it seems.   With glee

The unburied giants of old Cumbria wear

On their huge shoulders their death drapery—

The pall of snow.   Wide Morecambe sands are

     bare,

But sparkle, as if strewed with dust of diamonds rare.

2.

All things are bright, though silent.   Overhead

There is no cloud : 'tis one deep vault of blue

That mocks the eye to gauge it.   If, instead,

I look upon the waters, without clew

Or rod, for measurement, I am : I view

The boundless still ; and still within me rise

The old, old baffled thoughts I yet pursue,

But can achieve no end.   Oh, for new eyes

Of Mind, to pierce the deep, the eternal mysteries !

3.

I had a friend, in youth, I loved full well.

He was no mannikin—no dapper thing

That smirks, and reckons Life a bagatelle ;

But girt the bow of his mind with steely string,

And shot far after Truth—within the ring

Oft planting his arrow where her jewels glow,

All-priceless.   Humble in birth, he was a king

In thought.   I see his broad Baconian brow

Brighten, as mind-fire flashes in the eyes below ;

4.

I hear his manly tones announce the clear

Decision he had raught, when we the fray

Dialectic,—stern, unbending, and austere,—

Had waged for hours. And now I hear him
  say—

They were his dying words—for soon the clay

That glorious spirit left: " Oh, how I long

To be all intelligence!" Thus did he pray

In death : prayed from the passions' blinding throng

To escape for ever, that on Truth, with vision strong,

5.

For ever he might gaze : with spiritual eye—

The eye unlensed, unorganed, unbeshrined

In flesh, undimmed by vulgar slovenry

Of earthly use. He prayed that as pure Mind

He might exist : not only unconfined

By shroud o' the flesh, but unannoyed, unstained

By the foul cleavings of all humankind

To the earth, which do convince the soul, sore-
  pained,

That, while on earth, unto the grovelling clay 'tis
  chained.

6.

Hath he his dying wish obtained in death—
That is, in the real life beyond the grave?
For, since 'tis not the kernel perisheth,
But only the shell, one cannot choose but crave
To know what kind of life our spirits have
Unclothed upon with flesh.   Doth he still see—
Hear—feel?   Or, did the senses but enslave
And dull the soul's perceptions—while, now free
From sense, she is Perception's self—the destiny

7.

My dying friend aspired to—and now he
Is "all intelligence"?   Yet, often he said,
In our tense arguings, that it could not be
For any mere creature to have being unwed,
To vehicle, or clothing : only the Dread,
All-infinite One could be pure Mind.   And then,
If I asked—"How such thought-realms can we
   tread?"
He quoted Cudworth—whose intellectual ken
He deemed the strongest of all late Platonic men.

8.

And thus men quote, and reason still—or guess;
But get no farther!
   Yon big cumulus cloud
Hath suddenly risen from some lake's recess,
To hide the lordliest mountain in its shroud;
And Coniston Old Man, that looked so proud
Above his fellows, is invisible—
While more clouds pile upon the obscurer crowd
Of peaks, and make them seem to bulge and swell
Till they in stature Alps or Andes would excel.

9.

Let me leave clouds and mountains, for the sea!
Our reasoning is but rasher guessing, full
Of fancied peaks from which immensity,
We think, at last, we fathom.   We are dull
Scholars in learning how to pick and cull
True treasure from the trash of our own thought.
All reasoning on the eternal future null
And void must be.   What God hath left untaught
About it must be best unknown, or left in doubt.

10.

Let me breathe freely thy fresh air, glad main!

And, thankful, gaze upon thy boundlessness—

What, though I try to measure thee, in vain?

He measureth thy waters—measureless

To man—in the hollow of His hand!   Transgress

Thy bounds thou canst not; neither can I mine.

It will be wisest for me to repress

Guesses about the Future, and resign

My soul with confidence into the Hand Divine!

11.

I thank Thee, Lord, the days of arrogance

Are past, when I presumed Thy government

Divine to arraign: with rash precipitance,

Forbidding Thee to punish sin unblent

With blame of Thine own creatures, on earth sent

To do Thy will, but given to have a will

Themselves.   I thank Thee that the veil is rent

Of pride; and, since Thou only know'st how ill

It is in man to sin—his span of life to fill

12.

With base ingratitude for all Thy care

Perpetual, all Thy love unwearied,—new

Ever, each night and noon and morn,—I dare

Not judge what sin deserves.   Thou only true

And righteous judgment canst pronounce, whose

    view

Is blinded by no error, and whose right

It is to judge.   That punishment is due

To baseness here, men doubt not : to requite

The lawless, would on law and justice be a blight.

13.

Man's teachers now are saying, on every hand,

What I once rashly said and sung—that pain

And punishment cannot be ever : bland

And bountiful and tender, doth Thy reign

In Nature Thee proclaim ; and every grain

Of Gospel truth is sweetened with Thy love :

Thou canst not punish ever, and the stain

Of evil from Thy holy throne above

For ever see—men say : it would Thy being disprove !

14.

Vast Sea! how little of thy compass can

I judge from this scant spot on which I look

Upon thy waves!　And can it be that Man,

The slave of sin—from his dim finite nook—

Doth claim to read, off-hand, the eternal Book—

The Book of the infinite government of God?

Surely, Unerring One, Thou dost not brook

That men, unblamed, should thus assume the nod

Divine—should thus forget their kindred with the

　　clod!

15.

Farewell, grand Sea! I may not soon upon

Thy waters look again, and try to read

Thy healthful lessons.　Hence, I must begone,

Away from silence, to the crowds who lead

Their lives in noise and haste, and greatly need

Patient and thoughtful guidance from the way

Of Error to the paths of Truth.　Lord, speed

Me in my aim to spread Thy Truth, I pray—

For soon I shall have lived, to the end, my little day!—

16.

I left the realm of silence by the Rail.

There was no Rail whereon the steam-steed sped

With snort, and puff, and haste to turn men pale

With fear, and fill their hearts with instant dread

Of death, when I was young.   But, steady tread

Of waggon-horses, stout and strong ;—the dash

Down hill and up, o' the mail, without a shred

Of fear, to coachee's chirrup—not the lash

O' the whip ; the cheery horn ; no dread of deathful

   crash !

17.

"Oh, for the dear old coach again ! " I cry—

But soon remind myself o' the pelting rain,

And that umbrella which the old man would try

To hold up still for shelter, with insane

Resolve, although it drenched our necks ; the pain

Of sitting, crampt, for lack of room ; the wind

That kept us in one posture, like a chain—

It was so keen !   And then I am inclined

To own 'twas well men did the steam-steed find, and

   bind !

18.

I left the realm of silence, and arrived,

Once more, i' the realm of noise, and haste, and toil:

The realm of cotton mills, in which seem hived

Man, woman, child : all join the gainful moil,

'Midst heat, and rattle of machines, and broil

Of steam.   And still they build new mills, and vaunt

That nought their enterprise shall henceforth foil

Until their manufactures spread aslant

The world—where'er is found the human habitant !

19.

But thirty years ago, Lancastrian land

Was filled with discontent ; and ghastly fear

Prevailed the Poor would seize the pike and brand,

Through hunger-bitten madness, and ungear

The chariot of the State, and Order sheer

Overboard cast into the abysmal flood

Of universal ruin.   Many a seer

Proclaimed that revolution, battle, and blood

Must come, if men and women and children had not
food.

20.

How the sage holder of the reins displayed his skill,

And starving crowds gat food, there is no need

That I should tell.   When hungry men could fill

Their stomachs, they soon ceased to list the rede

Of agitators.   "Let us work, and feed

And clothe ourselves and children," soon became

The all-prevalent resolve. They worked with speed.;

And when broke out, across the sea, the flame

Of war, and they could get no cotton, they did not

   blame

21.

The "Cotton Lords," of whom, in bygone time,

They spoke so angrily.   Their common sense

Kept them from insurrectionary crime ;

And, famine-stricken though they were, suspense

Of work and wage with patience most intense

Was borne.   And, now the wheels go round

Again most merrily, thoughts of turbulence

Return not—for men's eyes upon the ground

Are fixed: to thoughts of food and clothes their minds

   are bound,

22.

Except where curse of gambling hath possest

The souls of men and women—for, to share

This madness of their husbands, with wild zest,

Women are found !   No more, i' the open air,

I see, at eve, pale, eager groups, with rare,

Though homely eloquence, holding debate—

Their heads unhatted, and their lank limbs bare

Of clothing, save with rags—far on, till late

Dusk hour : and still they lingered to deliberate

23.

How freedom should be won, and man be ruled

As man, by his own free choice, not as a slave !—

And hath the fervent thirst for freedom cooled ?

" You see the ragged crowds no more!"—with brave

Display of triumph, they proclaim, and wave

Their new-bought hats !   Most gladly I discern

The rags are gone ; but sorrowfully crave

Whither had fled the intelligence, and stern

Passion for freedom with which once they seemed to

yearn—

24.

The starving "Mill-hands?" Was thy word, then,
  true—
Sage Age-fellow Illustrious, that—spite all
The cry and rage and threat against the Few
That rose from the Many—'twas not to disenthrall
Themselves from serfdom, but to make their call
And shriek of hunger heard till they were fed?
'Twas all that Chartism meant; and now the tall,
Grim scaring spectre flees—for men have bread
To the full; and all their say for Freedom they have
  said!

25.

Then, from my inmost soul, I sorely grieve
That I and others bore for such as ye—
The grovelling sons of sires who could upheave
The world with fear—whose rags, so vile to see,
Were robes of honour, for they were the fee
Of independence!—sorely grieves my soul
We bore the chain for such as bow the knee
To Pelf and Privilege, so that the dole
To work for wages they may have. Is this the goal

26.

Of Freedom? Have ye reached it, then, so soon?
And now, with hands in pockets, ye can prate
Of shares in stores and building clubs; and—boon
'Bove all!—can bet on horses—like the great!
Or, on the flight of pigeons; or, elate
With idiot pride, lead greyhounds in a string,
And bet upon the swiftness of their gait!—
For, now, all's well! With scorn, aside ye fling
Fantastic Freedom, and vote the way sure bread to
   bring

27.

Into your cupboards! Ye are men of sense:
Your ragged sires were fools, and dreamers wild.
Freedom to feed ye prize: with abstinence
And Liberty ye cannot be beguiled;
For ye have tasted bread, and said, and smiled,
"'Tis sweet, and we will keep it. Take our vote
And welcome! Rule with hands clean or defiled,
So long as we can feed to the full. A groat
We care not how ye rule: on that we spend no thought!"

28.

And did we brave the dungeon, but to know

That toiling men have sold their birthright, like

Esau of old, for a mess of pottage? Low,

Indeed, your starving sires, who talked o' the pike,

Would say their well-fed sons had sunk! Heart-sick

To see such degradation, they would be,

And cry—"Ye strike for wage—but why not strike

For Freedom? Ye who have the vote, like free

Men use it: your own hands now hold your destiny!"

29.

My hour of teaching came; but there came few

To listen of the hands-in-pockets crowd:

They flocked to gaze upon some gew-gaws "new

From Lunnon!" I to my lodging with a cloud

Of moody thinkings paced——

               Hush! hush! the shroud

They are preparing for the breathless clay

That held the noblest soul on earth! No proud

Large-acred duke, or gartered marquess they

Adorn with heraldry, and clothe with Death's array.

30.

" The great Triumvir," saith the printed sheet
Of evening news, " hath died at Pisa."   Fame
Shall now reverse her trumpet, and, with meet
Proclaim, speak of an actor in the drame
O' the Nineteenth Century, whose high-souled aim
None equalled.   And Italia's passionate heart
Shall sob with penitence, and throne the name
Of her Mazzini far above the smart
And courtly names of men that played their part

31.

Of seeming patriotism, for kings to win
Continuance of their sceptres.   Ay, 'tis night
With the poor lifeless clay : shrunken and thin
It lies, no doubt! Quenched are those lamps of light—
Those " windows of the soul "—so dazzling bright
When it looked through them, while he thought and
    spoke   .
Of home !—so full of splendour and of might,
When from his eloquent lips the syllables broke
Of fair Italia fully freed from foreign yoke,

32.

And then united : Tuscan, Piedmontese,

Roman, Venetian, and Sicilian land,

All one freed home for patriot hearts at ease !

Old feuds now mourned ; and thrown away the brand

So often drawn to shed with brother's hand

A brother's blood !   The worn, thin clay is cold

And lifeless—but, I dare be sworn, 'tis grand

In death ! No soul e'er left a nobler mould ;

And still, I doubt not, it is beauteous to behold !

33.

How glossy were his raven locks when first

I saw that classic head !   But when I saw

Him after his return from Rome—the worst

Having befallen his rule, from the fell paw

Of France—and while I gazed, with sorrowing awe,

Upon his face, I marked his head was gray !

I spake on't—but it only served to draw

A smile from him : " We watched, by night and day,

While Garibaldi and our Romans kept the fray "—

34.

He calmly said—"with the French and Oudinot.

I never slept on a bed, and only ate

Dry bread and raisins, while they met the foe ;

And Saffi, and I, and Armellini, sate

To mete out justice—or deliberate

What next to essay.   The Corsican's false heir

Hath blasted our fair hopes.   But better fate

Awaits us.   Never, my friend, can I despair :

Our cause shall yet, in Rome, victorious laurels wear!"

35.

Where shall his tomb be ? In Santa Croce's fane,

Where sleep the grandest of Italian dead ?

Mazzini's bones were worthy to be lain

By the bones of Angelo, the sculptor dread,

Or Galileo's—but his final bed

Should be in Rome.   She was the darling dream

He cherished ; Popeless Rome become the head

Of Italy : her beauty, again, the theme

Of all ; and crowned with her loving People's diadem !

36.

Oh, honour the dead clay, Italians, for

The sake o' the soul that wore it !   Honour well

The clay, for the soul's sake ; but homage more

The lofty memory of the man !   Oft tell

Your children how he toiled, amid the swell

Of tyrant rage, and failure of his plan,

So oft renewed, the Austrian's pride to quell,

Freedom restore, and Italy in the van

To place, of nations : the Great Realm Republican !

37.

Say how he toiled and never fainted ; nor

His toil gave up till death ! So deep, so true

Was that great love to Freedom which he bore, ·

And to his darling Italy !   Ever grew

The affection with his years.   He never knew

An ebb and flow of that great love.   'Twas one

With his own being : a love that did imbue

And colour all his thoughts, and give them tone :

He lived and breathed in that great love, supreme,

    alone !

38.

Champion of " God and Duty"—for they were
Thy watchwords—who shall now the counsels guide
Of Freedom ?   Only one true arbiter
She needs : the Man of Equity.   Low Pride
That pulls down higher Pride—setting aside
One wrong to plant another—doth but breed
New troubles, and impede the gladdening stride
Of Freedom.   Had poor France but taken heed
To thy sage chiding, she had now been free indeed.

39

Farewell, grand Soul !   Rienzi meets thée there,
In Christ's bright heaven—the heaven of truthful
    souls—
With Brescian Arnold, and the man of prayer,
The martyred Savanarola : men, i' the rolls
Of Papal Rome, set down to share the howls
Of the accurst.   Thank God, nor Pope, nor Priest,
Shall be our judge !   'Tis He alone controls
Our destiny.—Grand spirit, take thy rest
With Him and Christ, in the sweet regions of the Blest !—

40.

Midnight hath found me pondering, once again,

The change of earthly things.   One cannot hear

That great ones die, and pass it by, as men

Pass by the deaths of every day—no tear

Shedding, or heed vouchsafing to the drear

Dull tale.——

        I slept again—the sleepless Mind

Still of her waking thoughts keeping a clear

And vivid hold—and seemed to tread the assigned

Realm of the Lord's beloved, whom evil men maligned

41.

And martyred. By the winding river I seemed

Again to walk ; but ere I stooped to take

One growth of that sweet floral land, I dreamed

The forms I kenned of two that, while awake,

I thought of sorrowfully.   One of them spake

With the bold martyr who to fiercest flame,—

By cunning of the Pope he caused to quake,—

Was doomed at last : the Pope whose English name

Was Breakspear : none more skilfully played the Papal

    game.

42.

Girolamo Savanarola told his heart,

In Paradise, with forceful yet with meek

And gentle speech. Arnold of Brescia's[1] part

Was sterner. As, in life, he never sleek

Or servile features wore, or uttered weak

And wavering words, so now he seemed to look

And speak as one who lived in days antique,

And lineage claimed with men who could not brook

The thought of slavery, much less bear its hateful yoke.

43.

Truly Italian souls they were. Their inward fire

Of patriotism was equal. One had learned

To mitigate his speech, so that no ire

Was e'er suspected. In the other yearned

O'er Italy a soul that often burned—

Some hastily said—with flame that made them fear

It was unchastened. But the pure discerned

No sin in all his warmth. Thus, oft, sincere

And fervid souls are judged with judgment too austere.

44.

" They flung thy ashes to the Tiber," said

The Florentine,² " and to the Arno mine ;

And soon the sea commingled and outspread

Them o'er the globe. And so each foul design

To frustrate Freedom fails !   Though to confine

And stifle her life-giving breath they strive,

Men's strife but serves to spread her breath divine

Till slayes inhale it, and restorative

Proclaim her power to every enslaved soul alive !

45.

" Kingship—that we ne'er loved—still lives, 'tis true ;

But our loved Italy owns no despot sway.

And, were it not for Loyola's cunning crew,

The Papacy would soon see its last day.

Oh, surely, on the march of Freedom, may

We now congratulate each other, while

We laud the Almighty Ruler.   Though His way

Be in the clouds for ages, they shall smile

With joy, who watch with patience how He works

His will ! "

46.

"My joy is feebler, brother, than thine own,"

The elder martyr spake : " I long to see

Our countrymen unto full manhood grown,

In thought and act.   Scarcely from childhood, we

Can say they have passed, while many a devotee

Climbs on his knees the Santa Scala,³ day

By day ; and, when the baby effigy

Of Christ—the doll Bambino⁴—on its way

To the sick is seen, Italian women kneel and pray,

47.

"I' the open street.   How can men call our land—

Our Italy beloved—except in whim—

A land of Christ, who died that we might.stand

Acquitted in the Father's sight ?   The hymn

They raise to Mary, Queen of Seraphim,

And Mother of. God—not to the Crucified !

' Ora pro nobis ! '—how their voices swim,

Yet, in our spiritual ear !   When last we hied

On our Lord's errand, and again beheld the pride

48.

"And pomp of their false worship, and the throng's

Profanity, beneath that stately dome,

How burned our minds with sense o' the Saviour's wrongs

Inflicted in our loved Italian home !

If Christian martyrs of old pagan Rome

Could rise, and see what priests call worship, in

Yon proud basilica, that still the gloom

Of heathenism prevailed—the gloom and sin—

They would declare : so near to heathenism akin

49.

"Is popish worship !   Oh, that God would bring

To nought the guilty system, and restore

His Son's pure truth !"—

　　　　　" To the Eternal King

Be fullest praise that on the Italian shore

Men scatter Gospel seed !   The Christian sower

Is free to come; and bring the Bible, too !

Doubt not, Italians, now they are free to explore

Its truths, will soon, intelligently, the true ·

Discern, and faith in their old priestly frauds eschew."

50.

Thus Savanarola strove the overhaste
To check that Arnold felt.   But now drew near
A band of Italy's martyrs of the Past:
Arnulph,[5] the holy preacher, bold, austere,
In time of Pope Honorius, who with fear
Filled hearts of cardinals and priestly knaves:
With fear—not penitence: they shed no tear ;
But seized him, nightly, by the hands of slaves,
And silenced his bold preaching in the Tiber's waves.

51.

With him came Martin Gonin, and Varaille,
And Nicolas Sartoire, and Pierre Masson,[6]
And hundred martyrs more, from many a vale
Of Piedmont: poor Vaudois barbes, so long
Exposed, with their devoted flocks, to wrong
From popes, and priests, and Dominic's black band.
Next came Mathurin,[7] and his wife so strong
In faith, who cried "Don't yield! give me your
    hand!"
And walked with him to burn, with fortitude so grand !

52·

Of northern Italy these : the southern clime—

The sunny Naples—had its victims, too :

Apulians, and Calabrians, who no crime

'Gainst man committed ; and to God with true,

Humble, and faithful hearts they lived.   But who

Could 'scape the Inquisition's deadly gaze ?—

They butchered eighty men with the knife: they slew

·Them as his sheep or swine a butcher slays,

Cutting their throats, in turn.   And ere they gave to
the blaze

53·

Their female victims, sixty were tortured till

Some died o' their wounds.   Nor did Venetia proud

Escape the Inquisition's yoke.   Its various skill

In killing men and burying them was shewed

In Venice : the victim needed no expense of shroud :

Tied fast upon a plank, a stone at his feet,

Between two little gondolas they rowed

Him to the outer harbour : then, with fleet

Motion, the boats withdrew ; and without a winding-
sheet

54.

Their victim found a grave in the lagoon.

Giulio Ghirlanda,[8] calling on the Lord,

Thus sank to death ; Ricetto,[9] next ; and soon

Spinula,[10] and Fra Baldo :[11] the record

Of all the names were long to tell.   Reward

In Paradise these found, and to embrace

Their brother martyrs came.   O'er the green sward

And flowery vale, in crowds, they trode apace,

While high and holy gladness shone in every face !

55.

What famed Italian city had not there

A martyr for Christ's unadulterate faith

'Twere hard, indeed, to tell.   Florence the fair

Had many besides Girolamo to death

Who bravely went.   And many the martyr's wreath

In Parma, Mantua, and Bologna gained ;

Or in Ferrara took the fiery path

To heaven ; or, while fierce Spanish Philip reigned,

In Milan, boldly in the flames Christ's truth main-
tained.

56.

Whence came the chiefest hundreds of that host?

Even from the spiritual Babylon. 'Twas Rome,

Herself, that fierceliest kept the demon boast

Of zeal in bringing heretics to doom,

By fire, or sword, or rack, or cord, or gloom

And hunger and silence of the prison cell.

Who thirsted most for blood, in Christendom ?—

For blood of Christ's own saints? The tyrants fell

Who boasted that they kept the keys of heaven right

   well !

57.

Their greetings o'er, I saw the martyrs group

Together, for discourse of what they saw,

Of late, on earth ; and of their faith, or hope,

That popish frauds would cease to overawe

Their countrymen, and Christ's pure truth be law,

Alone, unto their consciences. Of brave

Aspect, Bartoccio[12] soon began to draw

A crowd around him : he who was seen to wave

His hand, and heard to shout "Vittoria!" when they

   gave

58

His comely body to the flames, at Rome.

" Italian brothers, who love Christ ! "—so spake

The noble martyr ; " in our ancient home

We see the dawn, at length, begin to break

Of that thrice happy day, when old, opaque,

Benumbing errors of the soul shall fade

Like mists before the sun—when men shall wake

And cast off Superstition's dreams, dismayed

No longer by the hideous forms such dreams pourtrayed.

59.

" What, though Italians linger somewhat, yet,

To dash in pieces the false shapes that long

Enthralled their fathers' souls ;—to break the net

Of Loyola fully from off their limbs with strong

And manly effort ?   We shall hear the song

Of triumph soon, o'er Jesuitism and lies.

The Book of Christ's own truth is now among

Them : it lies open to enquiring eyes :

The Evangel shall, itself, our land evangelise !

60.

" There is no preacher like the Bible's self.

The living teacher is but human, like

His kind : he may be swayed by love of pelf,

Or pride ; or may be led astray by sick

Fançies that oft mislead even politic

And sober men.   The Book will ne'er mislead.

'Twill win its own grand way.   Full soon the trick

Of frighting men from reading it shall breed

A proud resolve from frown of priestcraft to be freed.

61.

" All hail the happy day, when earnest men

And women too, on all the Italian soil,

Each day by day, and hour by hour, with ken

Of humbleness, and prayer, and spiritual toil,

Shall 'search the scriptures,' and thus find the foil

To baffle, effectually, the guileful game

Which priests so long have played, and end the spoil

They have made of human souls i' the holy name

Of Christ!—Oh, holy Lord, cut short their reign of

   shame ! "

62.

"Amen, amen!" responded the rapt crowd—
"O Lord, subvert the soul-benumbing power
Of priestcraft, in our noble land!"—aloud
They prayed—"Thine own apostles trod its shore;
Thy martyrs bled upon the sanded floor
O' the Colosseum; the cities' streets engrained
Have been with many a Christian martyr's gore;
Our mountains and our vales their blood hath
　　stained!
O Lord! to our loved land restore their faith
　　unfeigned!"

63.

"And my soul saith 'Amen,'" the Brescian said;
"But what, if God to answer prayer delay—
Prayer scarce accordant with His purpose dread,
Or not yet ripened, so that they who pray
Can say they know it? He, in sovereign sway,
May humble Italy still more;—confound
Her national councils;—bring to low decay
Her wealth and strength. So long the craven hound
Of Austria, unto Prussia next she may be bound.

64.

"Oh, who can think upon her worldly glory—

Her old, great names of conquest and renown—

Her names of patriotism, so bright in story !

Her names of eloquence—the names thick strown

O'er history's pages—they that wear the crown

In Art, and Song, and Music—and not sigh

To see Italia sit with face half-prone

To the dust, and with half-folded hands—while sky,

And earth, and sea, resound with the awakening cry

65.

"Of new-born nations who aspire to be

A something in the scale, when worth is weighed,

And rank assigned 'mong men ?   Her ancientry

Would blush to see of what poor stuff are-made

Her modern men—mere men of masquerade :—

Except the few now leaving earth—the few

So far above the rest, each seems a shade

Of some old worthy which her soil upthrew

When naturally, it seemed, there glory and greatness

grew !"

66.

" My brother Arnold"—Savanarola spake,

With haste, and yet with tenderness, " we are all

Italians, and thy words, as a trumpet, wake

Our passionate love for Italy !   Yet fall

Thine accents on our incorporeal

And auditory sense, as if they told

Thy heart were more upon yon earthly ball

Than here, in Jesu's heaven"——

                           " My brother, hold !"

Cried Arnold ; " think me not, I pray thee, overbold

67.

" When I avow my spirit's love intense

For earthly themes, though far below the worth

Of heavenly.   Yet, I hear with reverence

Thy meek reproof.   For here, if not on earth,

The holier soul should have what elder birth

Claims there : brethren's obedient love."—

                          " I join

With thee, Bartoccio," Arnulph said ;—" 'Tis dearth

Of knowledge stops the way.   The Book divine,

If once Italians search with earnestness, no shrine

68.

" Of the Madonna shall find worshippers.

Before the gaudy rags with which priests dress

Her images, women shall cease to rehearse

Their prayers, and haste devoutly to confess

Christ Intercessor, by whom, alone, access

They have unto the Father. And the crime

Of years shall end : the crime of heinousness,-

That set up Mary as a means to climb

To heaven, shall never more be heard of through all

time !"—

69.

At once, Italia's myriad martyr host

I saw, lift up their hands, and cry, in prayer—

" Lord God Almighty, if one holocaust

Of martyrdom the vengeful Papal slayer

Could make of all our bodies, did we wear

Them once again, on earth, we would with joy

Crowd to the flames—yea, clap our hands, and bear

Them with a shout,—would it the vile alloy

Of Mariolatry with Christian truth destroy !

70.

"Lord, let Thy servant's prophecy be soon

Fulfilled !   Let sickly sentiment no more

Be misnamed piety ; nor crawling homage done

To Mary be miscalled devotion.   Pour

Thy light upon our loved Italian shore—

Thy holy light into Italian mind—

Until their mid-age darkness men abhor ;

And, seeing how Superstition did them blind,

Regard it as the foulest foe of human kind ! "—

71.

Forthwith, a venerable sight I saw

Of ancient martyrs from Italian land,

That seemed their brother martyrs' gaze to draw

As they approached.   No sons of Hildebrand,

Or Innocent, or Urban proud.   The band

Lowly and meek, they were, that Pagan hate

Drove to the catacombs ; and thence trepanned,

Full oft, to murder them.   A throng more late

I' the world's record came with them : sharers of like fate,

72.

And sharers of their lowly meekness too ;

But hugely varnished in the midnight time

That followed, as saints and miracle-workers true—

Some of them Roman bishops, ere a crime

Had stained the name of Pope ; and some in prime

Slaughtered of maidenhood—young virgins fair ;

And others of their sex, in age.   Sublime

In bravery, they did the fiercest tortures **bear,**

Until their torturers faltered 'fore their courage rare !

73.

Popes Clement, Sixtus, Fabian, Felix, all—

With Lucius and Cornelius [13]—though none dreamed

Of it—all canonised !   The pretence tall,

" I am infallible," none made. · Each seemed

A child in lowliness.   A face that beamed

With beauty followed : Agnes,[14] the virgin whom

Shrewd Diocletian, when he falsely deemed

He could destroy Christ's truth, sentenced to doom,

With many more, filling his realm with fear and gloom.

74.

Laurence, [15] the victim of Valerian, slain

With tortures most ingenious and prepense ;

And Roman martyrs in a crowd, i' th' reign

Of reckless Commodus, for Truth's offence,

Driven to fierce deaths ; and more, pre-eminence

Of martyrdom beneath the bloody sway

Of Decius who obtained ; a throng intense

Suffering Maxentius caused, ere yet the fray

O' the Milvian bridge brought Constantine the victor's

    bay.

75.

And many slaughtered in Maximian's rage ;

And others by Severus' seeming word

Of fairness.   Boasting Italian lineage,

These, all the gladsome martyrs of their Lord,

Now joined in heaven upon the flowery sward,

A grateful army, mingling to commemorate

The sweetness of their bliss.   On earth abhorred

Of wicked men, they felt their afterstate

The sweeter: it was bliss full-blossomed, consummate

76.

And now, in happy groups—withouten note

O' the times in which they lived on earth—for here

'Twas true fraternity—though ages mote

Have rolled between their births—in groups of dear

And holiest friendship gathered, they gave ear

Unto each other how the errand sped

On earth, from which they had returned.   Austere

And brave, as when the forfeit of his head

He paid to Commodus, sage Apollonius[16] said—

77.

" On errand of our loving Lord, I stood,

Of late, near to the weary soul of one

Who long had struggled with the surging flood

Of his heart's doubts and fears.   Renown he won

In college studies, when a youth, and none

More welcome would have found if he the pale

Of Rome's apostate Church had entered.   Groan,

And ave, and tears, his sister did not fail

To offer to Madonna, ere she took the veil ;

78.

"And then the simple nun spent half her life
In praying Mary from the heretics' snare
To save her brother.   Home brought daily strife,
With father's ire, to Giulio,—mother's prayer
And passionate entreaty.   If to share
The fellowship of young or old he tried,
He gat no help, no solace : to beware
Of mortal sin, of dark presumptuous pride
They warned him : not one strove to cheer him : all
    to chide.

79.

"Young Giulio dare not fully tell his soul
To any mortal.   Unto God he made
His moan : to God alone!   The priestly scowl
Was on him in the street.   'Neath sun or shade,
The wistful maids who saw him inly prayed
Madonna to be saved from deadly stain
Young Giulio bore—their own confessors said.
He struggled with his doubts and fears in vain :
He dared not bow to Mary, nor false worship feign ;

80.

"And, with conviction of heart-sin, he shrank

From supplicating God with cheerful mind.

Could he have brought his burthen with a frank

And filial trust before the Lord—the blind

Had fully gained his sight. But fears had twined

Themselves so thickly with his doubts, his gaze,

In love, upon the Saviour of mankind

He dare not fix—in grateful love; or raise

To Him, in cheerful confidence, one note of praise.

81.

"He pondered o'er the old Waldensian book,

So long in secret kept—the page of light

That first his faith in Romish errors shook—

Until he shrank with horror at the sight

Of Rome's idolatries, and murderous spite

Shewn to God's people, and His Truth; and thought,

Not seldom, he would tell the truth outright—

Would own himself the foe of the Devout,

Misnamed; and cry Rome's creed was but a Tale of

Naught!

82.

" But soon, again, remembrance of his sin

Bereaved his soul of strength.   He dared not speak

Of others' sin, while yet he could not win

A sense of pardon for his own.   To seek

So great a boon aright, he feared—with meek

Distrust of his own power—he knew not how ;

And hourly prayed that God, who aids the weak,

Would strengthen him the way of life to know

And enter on it boldly, spite of every foe.

83.

" Our ministry—in answer to his cry—

The Lord vouchsafed unto him ; and, in deep

Dependence on our Guide Divine, the eye

Within we strove of blinding films to sweep,

And fix it on perception that to reap

In joy is promised unto them that sow

In tears.   Some strength he gained, but soon o'er

cheap

He deemed salvation was, by faith : with low

Prostration he must still, with tears, in secret, bow.

84.

"We dreaded, now, lest penance, and the scourge,

And all the false humility and vice—

Not virtue—wherewith monks affect to purge

Men's sins, should fill his fancy, and entice

Him to attempt himself to pay the price

Wherewith his Saviour had already bought

His soul, and ransomed it for Paradise.

Our dread grew gloomier, for his mind, o'erwrought,

Seemed sinking—when the Hand Divine deliverance
brought.

85.

"An English Christian—whom young Giulio met

Amid some ruins, where, to nurse his grief,

In solitariness, and 'scape the fret

And torment of being watched, i' the fall o' the leaf,

He wandered—courteously besought a brief

Historic reason, if young Giulio's lore

Were rich enough to give it,—like a reef

Of rocks the sea hath left far on the shore—

Why there lay ruins which such marks of beauty bore.

86.

"The question pleased him, for he knew each stone
And vestige well of Rome's rich treasure-heap
Of ruins.   And he pleased the stranger.   Flown
Was twilight, ere their talk was done.   No peep
O' the moon was yet : and, 'mid the dark, to creep
From stone to stone, they tarried—for the theme
The stranger touched made Giulio's spirit leap
With eagerness.   Denouncing Rome's dark scheme,
The English Christian showed how freely did redeem

87.

"Men's souls, He whom the Father's pitying love
From His own bosom gave.   Young Giulio's eyes
The darkness hid, and much his spirit strove
To hide its tempest—so long used to spies
And listeners—but, o'ercome with sweet surprise,
He told his secret.   Now, the stranger blessed
The hour the Guide Divine—who doth advise
His servants true—had led him to the quest,
Unknown, of one who panted for the Saviour's rest.

88.

" Experienced in the windings of the heart

And intellect—the wards o' the locks of thought

And feeling—the good stranger drew apart

The fastenings of young Giulio's mind ; upcaught

The meaning of his failure to be taught

The truth of Christ by th' old Waldensian book ;

And gave him—such the words—'a treasure fraught

With priceless wealth.' In his young hands he took

It, while his frame throughout with grateful tremor

    shook !

89.

" It was the Bible in his native speech.

God shone upon it as he read. In Rome,

Now Giulio doth, each day, Christ's gospel preach,·

Where'er a poor man opens his mean home

To let the word of life be heard. They come

And listen, stealthily or boldly, while

The preacher onward speeds ; and, readily, some

Ask for the Book, and buy it. With the smile

Of scepticism some hear ; and pass on to revile

90.

"For Doubt abounds: its name is legion.   Where
Hath Rome's old tyrant power 'mong men been felt,
And human souls a strong deliverer
Not sought in sternest doubt—scorning to melt
In tears, where men so long have bowed and knelt
In childish fears?   Doubt still abounds; but death
To doubt the Book in many hearts hath dealt.
'Tis seed-time yet.   The harvest comes, God saith.
We rest upon His word whose name is Truth, in
    faith!"

91.

To Apollonius, while he told his tale
Of sorrow and joy, some hundred audience lent;
And when he raught the end, they did not fail
To thank the Guide Divine.   Meanwhile upsent
Were songs of praise.   'Mid other groups were blent
Like laud and joy, as others told how fared
They, in their visits to old Earth.   Intent
All seemed on learning what they chiefly cared
To know: that faith increasingly by men was shared.

92.

Just as the Hand of Light again was seen,

And the glad myriads in due order filed

Across the vale, their march unto the green

And terraced mountains to begin,—it thrilled

My soul to see how that large army smiled

To see another Martyr band advance—

A glorious band—confessors undefiled!—

To join their brethren. Who were these? One glance

Sufficed to show they fell by Rome's intolerance

93.

In Piedmont, when rose the solemn hymn,

"'Venge, Lord, Thy slaughtered saints!" from Mil-

   ton's soul;

And Cromwell threatened English vengeance grim

That made the Pope turn pale, and stop the foul

And bloody massacre.   Mother with infant roll

They did adown the rocks: atrocity

The Savoy Duke endeavoured to control,

But could not.   The Pontifical decree

Was given in haste : Rome feared the fiat of the Free!

94

One noble heart came up with these, although
He died before them.   He who sang the song
Of Simeon, in the fire—" Now lettest Thou
" Thy servant, Lord, depart in peace ! "—So strong
The heart of man God makes to bear vile wrong !
Thus brave Bazana of Luzerna [17] died.
He doth to the black calendar belong,
Likewise, o' the Inquisition's murders wide
And deep.   Could blackest Hell itself their vileness
    hide ?

95.

The Martyrs of the Valleys, newly come,
Filed off in order for the march.   No peal
Of trumpet summoned them, no pipe, nor drum,
That rouseth men, on earth, to slaughterous zeal.
The beckoning Hand of Light to advance, or wheel
Guides them.   And on they move—Italia's host
Of Martyrs, on whom Rome set her strong heel,
To crush out life : a dreadful holocaust
To Evil !   Nor is her zest for murder changed, or lost—

96.

Though great Mazzini's life of labour served

To kindle fire of freedom in the breast

Of his "Young Italy"—and strongly nerved

Some earnest hearts to dare, and hands to wrest

A victory for freedom ; and the pest

Of Popery now hangs its head.   Oh, no !

Rome hath not changed.   Nor ever will men rest

Peacefully in Truth while she can work them woe.

Of Freedom and of Truth she is the deadliest foe !—

97.

I heard begin the tuneful swell of praise—

Soon changed to prayer for Italy—as on

The Martyr Army marched.   But soon my gaze

On their bright ranks grew dim; and faint the tone—

And fainter—of their chaunt.   Before the throne

The martyrs soon will bow, in rapture high,

I thought, as I awoke.   But, not yet done

Is my earth-labour.   I must better try

To live—"as ever in my great Taskmaster's eye."

[1] Stanza 42. ARNOLD of BRESCIA. His triumphant patriotism and mortification of Pope Adrian (Breakspear), with his fall and martyrdom by burning, at the command of the Pope he had humbled, are among the most romantic incidents of Italy's romantic history.

[2] Stanza 44. "The Florentine"—SAVANAROLA.

[3] Stanza 46. SANTA SCALA. "Nearly opposite the steps of the church of St. John Lateran, we saw the devout, or penance-performing worshippers, ascending the Santa Scala on their knees. This is a flight of stone steps, said to have been taken from the palace of Pontius Pilate at Jerusalem, twenty-eight in number. The strange spectacle of young and old, rich and poor, fat and lean, cheerful and sorrowful, slow and rapid, clumsy and agile, moving on their knees up those steps, must be seen to be understood. The contortions, the jostling, the groaning, the praying, the kissing the steps, the serious gravity of some, the anxious faces of others, the irresistible tumbling, and, consequently, ludicrous collisions occasioned by the sudden stoppages of others, render the scene mournful, or ridiculous, according to the state of mind of the observer."*

[4] Stanza 46. BAMBINO. "We visited the church of Santa Maria d'Aracœli. Here a monk showed us the far-famed *Bambino*, a swathed and dressed olive-wood image of the infant Saviour, encrusted with

---

* "Journal of a Tour in Italy, in 1850; with an account of an interview with the Pope at the Vatican." By the Rev. Geo. Townsend, D.D., Canon of Durham: page 91. Rivingtons, 1850. [Dr. Townsend was the antagonist of Sir Wm. Drummond, the author of "Œdipus Judaicus."]

jewels,—which they take, if requested, to the titled and opulent sick. A carriage, two hours after, was seen to receive it and return it. The women in the streets kneel as it is borne past them."—Page 97 of the same work.

⁵ Stanza 50. ARNULPH. "At this time (A.D. 1128) under Pope Honorius II., a certain priest, named Arnulph, came to Rome, a man of great devotion and a distinguished preacher. While he proclaimed the word of God, he rebuked the dissoluteness, the libertinism, the avarice, and the extreme haughtiness of the clergy. He exhibited, for universal imitation, the poverty and life of spotless integrity of Jesus Christ and his apostles. In truth, his preaching was approved by the Roman nobility, as that of a true disciple of Christ. But, on the other hand, it exposed him to the intense hatred of the cardinals and the clergy, who seized him by night, and put him to death secretly."— *Trithemius: quoted by Monastier.*

⁶ Stanza 51. MARTIN GONIN was but thirty-six years of age. He was sentenced to be drowned in the Isère, in Dauphiné. The sentence was executed in the night.—GEOFROI VARAILLE, aged fifty, was burnt at Turin, 1558.—NICOLAS SARTOIRE, a young student of Berne, was burnt at Aosta, in Piedmont, 1557.—PIERRE MASSON, a Vaudois *barbe*, or pastor, was waylaid on a journey, and arrested. He was put to death at Dijon, in 1530.—*Monastier.*

⁷ Stanza 51. MATHURIN: burnt at Carignan, in Savoy, in 1560. His wife found entrance to his prison, exhorted him to constancy in the presence of his judges, and offered to go with him to die, if they would give her leave: *They granted her request.—Monastier.*

⁸ ⁹ ¹⁰ and ¹¹ Stanza 54. GIULIO GHIRLANDA was the first who suffered martyrdom in the city of Venice. He sank into the deep, calling upon the Lord Jesus.—The next was ANTONIO RICETTO, a most honourable man. In the gondola he was firm, prayed for those who put him to death, and commended his soul to his Saviour.—FRANCIS SPINULA was drowned ten days after Ricetto.—The most distinguished of all the martyrs of Venice was FRA BALDO LUPETINO. He was of a noble and ancient family, became a monk, and rose to high rank in his Order. He was imprisoned twenty years by the Pope and the Inquisition,

and then put to death. He met his martyrdom with great firmness, and in peace.—"Sketches of Protestantism in Italy," by Robt. Baird, D.D., of New York.

[12] Stanza 57. BARTOLOMEO BARTOCCIO, son of a wealthy citizen of Castello, in the duchy of Spoleto. He was imprisoned, but escaped to Venice and thence to Geneva. In 1567, he was seized in Genoa, by the Inquisition, and sent to Rome, on the requisition of the Pope. "After an imprisonment of nearly two years, he was condemned to be burnt alive. With a firm step he went to the place of execution; and, whilst the flames were enveloping his body, the words *Vittoria! vittoria!* —victory! victory! were distinctly heard from his dying lips."—Dr. Baird, in the volume just mentioned.

[13] Stanza 73. Popes CLEMENT, SIXTUS, FABIAN, FELIX, LUCIUS and CORNELIUS. I would not deny to these primitive Bishops of Rome the rank of true martyrs.

[14] Stanza 73. AGNES, the Virgin: martyred at Rome, in 305. Jerome, Augustine, and Ambrose, join in praise of her virtues.—See Alban Butler's "Lives of the Saints."

[15] Stanza 74. LAURENCE. The circumstances of the martyrdom of Laurence, in A.D. 258, are often doubted. But if he really were roasted to death, over a slow fire, on a gridiron, I see no reason to doubt that the intrepid martyr, after suffering some time, should have defiantly bid his torturers to turn him on the other side.

[16] Stanza 76. APOLLONIUS, a Roman senator, was beheaded in the reign of Commodus, after defending himself before the Senate.—*Eusebius*, Book v., c. 21; *Jerome*, in his Catalogue of Illustrious Men; *Tertullian*; etc.

[17] Stanza 94. BAZANA of LUZERNA: a nobleman burnt to death at Turin, on the 23rd Nov., 1623. They bandaged his mouth, as he left the prison. "But, as the executioner was tying him to the stake, the bandage fell off, and the martyr thus proclaimed the cause of his death: —'People,' he said, 'it is for no crime I die, but for seeking to act in conformity with the word of God; to sustain truth against error; to—' Here the Inquisitors stayed him, by putting light to the pile. Bazana

set up the song of Simeon, as versified by Theodore Beza, that touching canticle sung by the faithful of his Church after the sacrament—

'Laisse— moi désormais
Seigneur, aller en paix'—

But his voice was soon silenced by the flames.' "—See " The Israel of the Alps : translated from the French of the Rev. Dr. Alexis Muston."— London : Ingram, Cooke, and Co. 1853.

Watson and Hazell, Printers, London and Aylesbury.

34
72
107
83
155
185
195
202
225
227

WORKS BY THE SAME AUTHOR.

THOMAS COOPER'S SERMONS.

SECOND THOUSAND.

PLAIN PULPIT TALK.

BY THOMAS COOPER,

Lecturer on Christianity, Author of "The Purgatory of Suicides," etc.

In Crown 8vo., price 5s., handsomely bound in cloth.

CONTENTS.

"Lord Shaftesbury said some time ago that he believed the most effectual means of dealing with the growing carelessness and scepticism of the working classes was to get members of their own class to go among them and preach the truth to them. From Mr. Thomas Cooper's 'Plain Pulpit Talk' we find that he has been for years carrying out this idea. And judging from these sermons, he must be a powerful influence. They are colloquial, yet full of matter; soundly evangelical, yet most strikingly illustrated; and he is not afraid to venture on familiar phrases. The whole volume is singularly direct and rousing."—*Sunday Magazine.*

"There is much genuine eloquence about them, and great truths and doctrines are clearly illustrated, sometimes in a very original fashion, but always well. We heartily commend Mr. Cooper's sermons to our readers; confident that they will enjoy the freshness of style and the characteristic force by which each and all are distinguished."—*Rock.*

"A very masterly series of sermons, from the heart and to the heart, remarkable for clear, vigorous language, and illustrations of the most clever and telling character."—*Standard.*

"No book ever better justified its title. These seven sermons, preached to tens of thousands all over the country, of which it consists, are full of homely, clear, and forcible 'talk' on the weightiest of themes. There is no mere rhetoric, much 'straight hitting' and practical directness. The language is the choicest Saxon, the illustrations are as racy as John Bunyan's, the style is as clear as the 'Pilgrim's Progress,' and the matter is full of the savour of the gospel of Christ. The book is full of reality. It fixes the attention, warms the heart, stimulates the intellect, and ennobles the life. These are words for the people by one who knows them, their difficulties and their needs, and who speaks not only with the authority of experience and of careful mastery of the subject, but also with the earnest sympathy of a friend."—*General Baptist Magazine.*

"The book before us answers exactly to its title; but while truly plain, these sermons are also racy, practical, and earnest."—*Wesleyan-Methodist Magazine.*

LONDON: HODDER AND STOUGHTON, 27, PATERNOSTER ROW.

THE BRIDGE OF HISTORY

OVER THE GULF OF TIME.

*A Popular View of the Historical Evidence for the Truth of
Christianity.*

By THOMAS COOPER.

Fcap. 8vo., 2s. 6d., cloth.

"The author gives a view of the historical evidence for the truth of Christianity which is at once clear and convincing, sound and just, popular and effective. His metaphor of history as a bridge goes beyond the title-page. He names every century, from the nineteenth to the first, by some characteristic man or event belonging to it, he calls it an arch, and each of these arches he traverses, from the nineteenth (the Arch of Science) to the first (the Arch of the Apostles), verifying as he goes, by incontestable facts, the existence of the belief of the facts which form the basis of the Christian faith."—*Evangelical Christendom.*

"When we first heard Thomas Cooper deliver the lecture which is now before us in a neat and really handsome volume, we thought we had never heard its equal. We are of the same mind still. It is the best popular exposition of the 'historical argument' by far that we have ever either heard or read."—*Day Star.*

"The present volume is in his best manner, and deserves to be scattered as men fling seed into the furrows, by handfuls. With God's blessing it will reclaim the sceptical and confirm the wavering."—Rev. C. H. SPURGEON, in the *Sword and Trowel.*

"Clearly written, and admirably enforced by strength of argument."—*Standard.*

"A clear and forcible statement, in admirably vigorous English, of the historical evidences that may be urged for the truth of Christianity. We warmly commend the book to teachers and others who have not time, or perhaps inclination, for the study of more elaborate works."—*Inquirer.*

"What has struck us most in the reading of the book is the fertility of the writer's intellect, which never seems to be overweighted with what lies beyond its immediate need, and yet never for an instant lacks a fact or an illustration. The moral and religious feeling of the whole is admirable—hopeful, buoyant, inspiriting."
—*Nonconformist.*

LONDON: HODDER AND STOUGHTON, 27, PATERNOSTER ROW.

THIRD EDITION.

THE LIFE OF THOMAS COOPER.

WRITTEN BY HIMSELF.

With a Portrait. Crown 8vo., 7s. 6d., cloth.

CONTENTS.

"The old man fights his battles over again with a vigour and enjoyment that can hardly fail to amuse and interest the readers of this stirring narrative. No one can read Mr. Cooper's autobiography without strong feelings of admiration and respect, or his 'Purgatory of Suicides' without recognizing in it creative imagination and true poetic fire."—*Spectator.*

"The book is an almost perfect illustration of a strange chapter of English history."—*Daily News.*

"Mr. Cooper is a man of remarkable powers, and he has had a remarkable history. The story of his life, which he has told with perfect frankness, and in clear, strong, picturesque English, is as interesting as a romance. No one who begins to read it will fail to finish it."—*Congregationalist.*

"It is as full of stirring incidents as a romance, and the easy, graceful manner in which the whole story is told is not the least of its merits. . . . The book is full of recollections of literary and political celebrities with whom the author came in contact at different times."—*Graphic.*

"This is one of the most entertaining pieces of autobiography in our language, crowded with incident and adventure. Great scholar, political actor, speaker, poet, sufferer, it is not possible such a life in its recital can be dull."—*Preacher's Lantern.*

"A most interesting volume."—*Leisure Hour.*

"Apart from its value as a political sketch, the narrative has such freshness and simplicity, and is written in such refreshingly pure English, that we recommend everybody to read it, and see how enthralling may be made the account of a life plainly told without polysyllables."—*People's Magazine.*

LONDON : HODDER AND STOUGHTON, 27, PATERNOSTER ROW.

SECOND THOUSAND.

In Crown 8vo., price 7s. 6d., cloth.

FAITH AND FREE THOUGHT.

Being a Second Course of Lectures

DELIVERED AT THE REQUEST OF THE CHRISTIAN EVIDENCE SOCIETY.

WITH A PREFACE BY

THE RIGHT REV. SAMUEL WILBERFORCE, D.D.,

Lord Bishop of Winchester.

CONTENTS.

SIR BARTLE FRERE on Christianity and Civilization.

The DEAN OF ELY on Pagan and Christian Society.

CANON BIRKS on Human Responsibility.

CANON MOZLEY on the Principle of Causation.

DR. ALLON on the Supernatural Character of Christianity.

DR. GLADSTONE on the Scriptures and Natural Science.

DR. ANGUS on Man a Witness for Christianity.

DR. BOULTBEE on Moral Difficulties of the Old Testament.

C. BROOKE, Esq., M.A., on the Order and Adaptations in Nature.

W. R. COOPER, Esq., on the Egyptian and Assyrian Monuments.

B. SHAW, Esq., M.A., on the Force Imparted to the Evidence of Christianity from the Manner in which a Number of Distinct Lines of Proof Converge in a Common Centre.

FROM THE BISHOP OF WINCHESTER'S PREFACE.

"The lectures are calm, sober, earnest, honest dealings with the several subjects they handle. These subjects cover the whole field of sceptical attack. We trust they will be found to have been calmly, truthfully, and convincingly handled by men worthy, by intellectual might, by knowledge of the times, and by their being thoroughly possessed with the truth of Christ, of dealing with such high arguments."

"The enemy is met boldly on his own ground, by adversaries skilful both in defence and attack, able to hold their own in all points of controversy, as men should who fight for the cause of truth."—*Standard.*

"An exceedingly valuable body of evidence in favour of our Christian faith."—*John Bull.*

"The whole of the lectures are worthy of a careful study."—*Leeds Mercury.*

"Open the book where you will, read a few pages, and the conviction that a liberal and thoughtful man is writing for those whom he expects to be liberal and thoughtful too, forces itself upon you. These essays display a boldness of admission, a fearless treatment, and, above all, a logic at once searching and cautious, which place them very high in the region of controversial theology."—*English Churchman.*

** *The Lectures may be had separately, price 6d. each.*

LONDON : HODDER AND STOUGHTON, 27, PATERNOSTER ROW.

www.ingramcontent.com/pod-product-compliance
Lightning Source LLC
Chambersburg PA
CBHW021056030726
47496CB00006B/1867